'You've got to be kidding.

'The Wedding Ring pact?' Despite everything, Hunter had to smile. 'You and your pals are certifiable—you know that, don't you?'

'Are we going to sit in this car all night?' Raven asked, wishing they were doing anything but sitting in neutral.

After a moment Hunter said, 'There's a quiet parlour in the inn where I'm staying. We can talk there.'

Her voice held a smile. 'You don't trust me enough to take me to your room?'

'It's not you I don't trust,' he muttered as he backed out of the parking space. 'I can't believe you can even joke about it, after the way I treated you last night.'

'What do you mean?'

'Just for the record, Raven, that wasn't my usual style. I wish I'd—' He sighed. 'Well, if it was going to happen, it shouldn't have happened that way. I wasn't thinking, I was just...I don't know what I was doing.'

'Well, whatever you were doing, it was pretty damn exciting.'

Dear Reader,

When four romantically minded school girls vow to find each other husbands if any of them are still single at age thirty, they have no idea how complicated it will make their lives twelve years later! Each of our matchmaking pals—Raven, Charli, Sunny and Amanda—will get her story over the next four months in THE WEDDING RING mini-series.

The pact is set into motion when Raven Muldoon's friends introduce her to Brent Radley. Brent is attractive, attentive and eager to tie the knot. If she could only stop obsessing about his sexy younger brother, Hunter—confirmed bachelor and owner of the local comedy club—she might be just as eager as Brent to make the relationship permanent. What can I say about the story you hold in your hands except...*Love's Funny That Way!*

Next month, look for *I Do, But Here's the Catch*, when Charli enters into a marriage of convenience that becomes decidedly inconvenient when she falls in love with her husband. In December you can read Sunny's story in *One Eager Bride To Go*, and finally, in January 2002, two-time divorcée Amanda, determined to remain single, tries to outwit her matchmaking friends in *Fiancé for Hire*.

I hope you'll join me for all four of these fun, sexy WEDDING RING stories. You can visit me on the Web at www.pamelaburford.com or write to me (include an SAE with return postage) at PO Box 1321, North Baldwin, NY 11510-0721, USA.

Love,

Pamela Burford

LOVE'S FUNNY THAT WAY

by

Pamela Burford

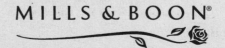

To Terry Biener, a sister-in-law who's more sister than in-law. Many thanks for sharing your expertise as a hypnotherapist.

*First published in Great Britain 2001
by Harlequin Mills & Boon Limited,
Eton House, 18-24 Paradise Road, Richmond, Surrey TW9 1SR*

© Pamela Burford Loeser 2000

ISBN 0 263 82820 4

21-1001

*Printed and bound in Spain
by Litografia Rosés S.A., Barcelona*

Prologue

Jones Beach, Long Island, August 1988

"CHECK OUT THE BUNS on that one." Amanda Coppersmith elbowed the dark-haired girl lying next to her on the tattered chenille bedspread that served as a beach blanket. "He's looking at you, Charli. Smile at him. Go ahead."

"Amanda, will you *stop?* He'll hear you!" Blushing through her deep summer tan, Charli Rossi dared a quick peek at the young man playing Frisbee several yards away.

On Amanda's other side, Sunny Bleecker rolled onto her stomach. She pillowed her head on her arm and pushed short auburn curls off her face. "Stop teasing her, Amanda. If you think that guy's so hot, go after him yourself." She grinned. "If you have the nerve."

"Is that a challenge?"

"I dare you."

"I double dare you," Raven Muldoon seconded, trotting up from the ocean, dripping wet. She dropped onto the blanket and butted Sunny with her hip. Her three pals scooted over to make room for her. "Who are we daring to do what?"

Charli leaned on an elbow. She whispered, "Sunny dared Amanda to talk to that cute guy."

Raven sat up and looked around. "Which cute guy?"

"Don't look!" Charli flipped onto her stomach and buried her face in her folded arms.

"The one in the neon green trunks," Amanda said, pointing.

"Nice buns." Raven pulled aside the shoulder strap of her multicolored racer-style swimsuit to check her tan lines. "I bet he's in college. Looks about twenty."

"An older man." A speculative gleam came into Amanda's eye. She tugged on her white bikini for the most alluring effect. "Maybe I *will* talk to him."

"Yeah, right." Raven reached into the cooler next to her for a cold can of diet cola. "You're almost as shy as Charli. You just talk big."

"Are there any Oreos left?" Sunny reached past Raven to paw through the tote bag crammed with snacks.

"What about you?" Amanda demanded of Raven. "I don't see you asking any guys out."

"I'm not shy," Raven said, releasing her ponytail and squeezing seawater out of her long, honey-colored hair. "Just discriminating."

"Yeah, that must be why none of us have boyfriends," Sunny drawled around a mouthful of cookie. "Because we are so very discriminating."

"What are you talking about?" Charli asked Sunny. "You have Kirk."

"*Had* Kirk."

Charli, Raven and Amanda exchanged looks of dismay.

Sunny sighed. She plucked another Oreo out of the package and just stared at it. Her customary joie de vivre seemed to have deserted her. "It's no big deal. Kirk's going to Stanford next week. I just started that waitress job at Wafflemania. We knew all along it couldn't last."

"But I thought..." Charli bit her lip. "I mean, I thought you really liked him."

"Sunny's right to call it quits," Amanda said, with her usual blunt pragmatism. "She just got a job here on Long Island. Kirk will be spending the next four years in California. Long-distance relationships are hopeless."

"I'm sorry, Sunny." Raven squeezed Sunny's shoulder, reaching out, as always, in empathy and compassion. "I was hoping you two could work something out."

"It's no big deal, okay?" Sunny hurled the Oreo onto the white sand and flopped back down onto her stomach. "It's not like we were that serious. I mean, he didn't even *ask* me to go out there with him. I guess he's looking forward to dating all those college girls." When no one said anything, she added, "Anyway, I won't be working at that greasy spoon for long. I won't have to— it's a great place to meet guys."

Amanda said, "And one of these guys is going to sweep you off your feet and you'll be engaged by Christmas."

"Hey, it could happen," Sunny said. "I bet I'll land a husband faster at Wafflemania than you will going to Cornell."

"But I don't *want* to land a husband!" Amanda said. "I want a career."

"Why can't you have both?" Charli asked.

"I'm not against marriage," Amanda said. "I'm just not fixated on it like Sunny is. We're young! We just graduated high school! Let's experience life before we think about settling down."

Sunny wadded up her T-shirt and shoved it under her head as a makeshift pillow. "I figure I'll really start experiencing life *when* I settle down with the right guy and we have a few kids. I want the kind of happiness my folks have. What's wrong with that?"

No one spoke for several minutes. A seagull swooped down to claim the Oreo. A pair of giggling children ran past, kicking sand onto the blanket. The girls sat up and passed around a tube of sunscreen, anointing their limbs and each other's backs.

Charli broke the silence. "We should help Sunny." The other girls looked at her questioningly. "I mean, we're her best friends, right? Getting married, having kids—it's what she wants more than anything. We should try to find someone right for her. It's how my grandma Rossi met my grandpa. Their families put them together, and they've been happy for fifty-seven years. Sometimes matchmaking works."

"Now I'm worried about both of you," Amanda said, glancing dubiously from Charli to Sunny.

Raven said, "I don't know, I think Charli has a point. How long have we all known each other?"

"Forever," Charli said, adjusting her modest one-piece swimsuit for maximum coverage. "Since kindergarten."

"So that's what?" Raven said. "Twelve years that we've been best friends."

"The Four Musketeers." Sunny's perennial smile was back in place. "That's what my dad calls us."

Charli started French-braiding Amanda's long, straight, pale blond hair. "My grandma Rossi calls us the *Club Nuziale*."

"What does that mean?" Amanda asked.

"The Wedding Club."

"Where'd she get that from?"

"I guess it's 'cause we're always talking about boys."

"And that means we have weddings on the brain?" Amanda rolled her eyes. "That is so old-fashioned."

"That's my grandma Rossi," Charli said with a fond smile.

Sunny leaned back on her palms. "Old-fashioned doesn't necessarily mean bad."

"The Wedding Club," Raven mused. "I kind of like that."

"Oh, no, not you, too!" Amanda threw her damp towel at Raven.

Raven tossed the towel aside and sat cross-legged, facing the others. "Or how about this? We're the Wedding Ring." She waited while her friends groaned at the double entendre, and added, "The thing is, we've been best friends forever. We've been through a lot together."

"Even Amanda's crush on Mr. Richards," Sunny teased.

"Hey, at least I never had a thing for Jimmy 'the Missing Link' de Luca," Amanda retorted.

The girls groaned even louder, and Sunny hollered, "I was twelve! I couldn't take my eyes off that brow ridge! Are you guys ever going to let me live that down?"

"We never told anyone else." Charli secured Amanda's French braid with a hair tie. "Our secrets are *secret*."

"The point is," Raven continued, "we've always been there for each other, no matter what."

"And we always will be," Sunny vowed.

Raven said, "We know we all want to get married someday. Some of us want to get married tomorrow." She gave Sunny a good-natured shove. "I like what Charli said about helping Sunny. I like to think we'd all pitch in and give that kind of help to any of us that needed it."

Amanda wrinkled her nose. "What are you talking about? Like playing matchmaker for each other?"

Raven's eyes lit with excitement. "That's exactly what I'm talking about."

"Give me a break," Amanda said. "We're not the kind of losers that need help getting dates."

The instant the words left her tongue, Amanda clamped her lips shut. But it was too late. In the charged silence that followed, no one looked at Charli, now seemingly preoccupied by the tufted pattern of the chenille beach blanket.

With gentle diplomacy Raven said, "Well, speaking for myself, there are times I can use all the help I can get."

"Well, speaking for *my*self," Sunny stated, "I'm not so desperate that I need someone else picking my husband. Talk to me when I'm twenty."

"So let's agree to do that," Charli said. "When Sunny turns twenty, if she's not married, not engaged or anything, the rest of us will find her a husband."

"Uh-uh." Sunny raised a palm. "This deal has to be for all of us. No way am I going to be singled out."

"Then it can't be age twenty," Amanda said. "I'll still be in college at twenty. And I'm probably going to graduate school after that."

"Twenty-five then," Raven said.

"No good. I need time to establish a career first." Amanda pulled on the oversize T-shirt that doubled as a beach cover-up. "Make it thirty or count me out."

Sunny laughed. "Thirty! All right, I'll help you guys find men when you're thirty. Maybe my husband and five kids will help."

Charli asked, "What if the one who's, you know, being matchmade doesn't like the guy the others choose for her?"

Raven gave it some thought. "Well...she has to give him a chance. A set period of time that she's got to keep seeing him, as long as he's interested."

"Even if he's, like, a pig?" Amanda asked.

"We're not going to set each other up with pigs," Sunny said. "We have to trust each other—like, even if you don't think the guy's anything special to start with, maybe your best friends, who know you better than anyone in the world, know better than you what you need."

"Or *who* you need," Raven added. "So how does three months sound? The one being set up has to go steady with the guy for three months before giving him the old heave-ho."

The others murmured agreement.

"Do we tell the guy he's part of a matchmaking thing?" Charli asked, clearly concerned about the technicalities, as if her turning thirty unmarried were a foregone conclusion.

"No way." Sunny shook her head vigorously. "I'd die of embarrassment. It's got to be done without him knowing."

"Why will *you* die of embarrassment?" Amanda asked with a smirk. "I thought you were going to be the one with the husband and five kids by thirty."

Sunny made a face at her.

Raven said, "We all have to agree to this pact. So think it over, everyone." She followed this immediately with, "Okay, time's up. Deal?"

"Deal," Charli said.

"I'm in." Sunny turned to Amanda. "How about it?"

"Oh, what the heck. It oughta be good for a laugh."

Raven thrust her arm toward the others, initiating the

group handclasp that had accompanied every solemn promise they'd made since kindergarten. Her friends followed suit, twining their fingers and holding firm.

"The Wedding Ring is hereby established," Raven intoned.

"Even though none of us will need it," Sunny added.

1

"IT WAS YOUR IDEA, Raven."

"How many times are you going to remind me?" Raven pushed away the heavy plate containing the crumbled remains of her corn muffin, and leaned her elbows on the table. She faced Amanda's smug grin straight on. "We were kids when we made that pact. Just out of high school. With stars in our eyes."

Amanda adjusted the silk scarf adorning the neckline of her cranberry-colored, wool crepe pantsuit. "You seemed pretty darn serious about it at the time. You took a solemn vow, if memory serves. And it was all your—"

"Don't say it again."

They occupied their regular table at Wafflemania, a square four-seater tucked into the corner of the non-smoking section. With her back to the door, Raven didn't notice Charli's arrival until she pulled out one of the empty chairs and dropped into it, still wearing her loden-colored wool overcoat.

The passage of years had mellowed Charli's plain, strong features. Right now, with her hair windblown and her cheeks pink from the cold, she could almost be called pretty, though Raven doubted Charli would ever think of herself as anything but Mr. and Mrs. Rossi's shy, homely youngest daughter.

"I would've been here sooner," Charli said, "but one of my symphonic band students needed help with a difficult piece."

"Raven's trying to weasel out of the Wedding Ring pact," Amanda said.

Charli gaped at Raven. "But we all agreed! We made a promise to each other! We've never broken our promises. Not ever."

"Nobody's breaking a promise. I just choose not to accept your help in finding a husband, that's all."

A hand appeared with a bulbous coffee carafe. "It doesn't work that way," Sunny said, as she expertly refilled Raven's mug. "You're not allowed to back out now."

"I don't recall that particular stipulation."

"I do." Sunny winked at her coconspirators. "You guys remember that part, don't you? Nobody's allowed to chicken out when it's her turn?"

"The 'chicken clause.'" Charli slipped out of her coat. "How could I forget?"

Amanda flapped her elbows and clucked her little heart out, drawing stares from other diners.

Raven groaned. "Why me?"

"Because you're the first one of us to turn thirty," Charli answered.

Amanda leaned back with a wicked grin. "Didn't think of that when you proposed this little scheme, huh? Did I mention it was all your idea?"

Sunny glanced around furtively—looking for her tyrant of a boss, no doubt—before perching on the edge of the vacant chair. Her sickly pink, polyester waitress uniform was as ugly and unflattering now as when she'd first stepped into it a dozen years earlier. Today it sported a coffee stain near the hem of the short skirt. Sunny's long, wavy auburn hair was secured in a braid that fell halfway down her back.

"Did you tell her about the guy?" Sunny asked.

"You picked someone already?"

"Amanda found him," Charli said. "He works with her."

"Wait a minute." Raven held her hands up as if to derail this runaway matchmaking train she'd set in motion. "I never agreed to this."

"Sure you did," Sunny corrected her. "Twelve years ago."

"His name is Brent Radley. He's the sales manager at *Grasshopper*," Amanda said, naming the children's magazine she published. "He's outgoing, fun-loving, not to mention—" she sent Raven a pointed look "—a stone hunk."

"If this guy's so great, how come you're not going after him yourself?"

"Two ex-husbands are more than enough for one lifetime, thank you very much."

"Who says you have to marry him?" Raven asked. "Just have some fun. Your last divorce was final two months ago. When are you going to start dating again?"

"When and if I start dating again, I intend to steer

clear of marriage-minded men. There's no way I'm walking down the aisle a third time."

"But the pact," Charli said.

"The pact is for those of us who *want* a husband," Amanda said. "In any event, Brent is thirty-four, never married, and I get the feeling he's thinking about finding that special gal and settling down. I told him about you, Raven."

"You didn't mention the Wedding Ring pact, did you?" Charli asked.

"Of course not. He just thinks I'm setting him up with a friend." She said to Raven, "He'll be at your place at seven-thirty. Dress casual."

"Tonight?"

"I didn't want to give you too much time to work yourself up over it."

"You set me up with a blind date? You know I hate blind dates!"

Sunny said, "Relax. You'll probably have a great time. Brent's the type to put you right at ease."

"He seems like a really nice man," Charli said.

"You two have met him?" Raven stared at her best friends. "You arranged this already, behind my back."

"Just give him a chance," Sunny said. "Hey, maybe you can hypnotize Brent to fall madly in love with you." She wiggled her fingers along her line of sight and spoke in a monotone. "You are growing sleepy. You have an irresistible urge to make a down payment on a five-carat diamond."

"If it were that easy, I'd have been married long ago.

Now, if this Brent wants to quit smoking or lose weight, then we're in business."

Raven had been a hypnotherapist for six years, operating a thriving private practice out of her home. She gained tremendous satisfaction using therapeutic hypnosis to help her clients improve their lives, whether their aim was to eliminate destructive habits, overcome phobias or simply improve their golf score.

From across the room, Sunny's boss, Mike, caught her eye and gestured impatiently at a table of new arrivals awaiting service. Sunny grumbled, "Hold your horses," and rose to her feet.

Raven sighed in exasperation. "All right. I'll give him a chance. One date."

"Three months," Amanda said. "As long as he's interested, you have to stick it out for three months. Now, who was it who suggested that rule? Oh yeah, wasn't it—"

"Just wait till it's your turn," Raven warned.

"Even if I were in the market for a husband, I'm last in line. Charli's next—she turns thirty in April."

Charli bit back a nervous smile. Raven reached across the table and squeezed her hand. Charli needed all the support and reassurance she could get.

"Then it'll be my turn." Sunny picked up the coffee carafe. "My birthday's July 1. You won't have to twist *my* arm."

"Do us a favor," Amanda drawled. "Don't book the reception till you've at least met the groom."

Mike started to stalk in their direction, prompting

Sunny to hightail it to the unattended table. But not before she'd muttered, "I can't believe I'm still working in this dump."

Raven slumped in her chair, wishing she'd kept her big mouth shut all those years ago.

"THIS IS A GREAT SPOT," Raven observed, glancing around the interior of Stitches, the comedy club Brent had brought her to. Their table was right next to the stage.

"I have connections," Brent said, with the warm smile she'd already become accustomed to in the half hour since he'd rung her doorbell.

Her pals hadn't been lying. Brent Radley was personable, relaxed and definitely—how had Amanda put it?—a stone hunk. Dark hair, blue eyes, six feet tall or a little over, lean and fit. He had the air of a man who knew he was attractive—usually a guaranteed turnoff. But he was also friendly and attentive, and Raven figured that was what really mattered.

She'd come to a decision as she'd changed outfits three times in nervous anticipation, finally settling on a long, pimento-colored silk dress topped by a beige crocheted vest. She'd decided that if her best friends in the world had gone to all this trouble for her sake, the least she could do was give the Wedding Ring scheme a chance. She'd worn a little makeup and carefully finger-styled her dark blond hair. Nowadays she wore it in a layered, chin-length cut with bangs, and on good days it framed her face in feathery, flattering waves.

The waitress stopped by their table, handed them menus and exchanged greetings with Brent, who was obviously a regular. She took their drink order and moved on.

The interior of Stitches was a delight. The dark-paneled walls were covered with framed story-magazine covers dating back to the 1920s. All genres were represented, from lurid detective rags to science fiction, adventure, western, and even confession magazines. An eclectic mix of tablecloths and mismatched dishes lent an air of homey mayhem. Soft bluegrass music underscored the burble of conversation and laughter. Tantalizing aromas drifted to Raven's nose: hot garlic bread, rich tomato sauce, fried calamari....

"I recommend the pizza rustica," Brent suggested, leaning forward to point it out on the menu. "It's called a personal pizza, but it's about the size of a hubcap." He spread his arms in illustration.

"Sold." Raven slapped her menu shut. The waitress returned with Brent's draft beer and Raven's mineral water, and took their dinner order.

"You said you have connections here." She sipped her bubbly mineral water. "Do you know the owner?"

"You might say that." Brent caught someone's eye and waved. "He's my brother."

Raven looked up to see a young man weaving among the tables toward them. He carried himself with smooth masculine grace and a proprietary air that told her who he was even before he stopped at their table and soundly thumped her date on the shoulder.

Without waiting for an introduction, Brent's brother turned to Raven and said with grave sincerity, "I want you to know how much our parents appreciate your agreeing to date this pitiful specimen."

She didn't skip a beat. "It was the least I could do after they posted bail for me."

An appreciative glint came into his eye, and Raven had the impression she'd passed some test. "You have his tranquilizers?" he asked. "Drool bib?"

"My trusty cattle prod's all I need." She patted the large shoulder bag hanging on her chair back. "That and a few brightly colored toys with round edges."

"Nothing with small pieces, I hope. You ever see a grown man cough up Barbie shoes? It's not a pretty sight."

Grinning, shaking his head, Brent said, "Are you two finished?" but his brother didn't even glance at him.

"I'm Hunter Radley." He extended his hand, and she shook it.

"Raven Muldoon." She was acutely conscious of the texture of his skin, the repressed strength in his firm grip. After a moment she made herself pull away.

The physical resemblance between the brothers was immediately apparent, although Hunter was obviously much younger. Both men had dark, wavy hair, but while Brent's was short and neatly trimmed, Hunter's brushed the collar of his ivory twill shirt. The shirt looked soft with wear, and the top couple of buttons were undone, revealing a V of skin dusted with dark hair. The same dark hair was visible on the forearms revealed by his rolled-up shirtsleeves. She noticed he wasn't wearing a wedding band.

"How did you get to be called Raven?" Hunter asked. "With a name like that, I would've expected black hair." He reached out to rub a strand of her honey-blond hair between his fingers. If any other man she'd just met had done that, she would have bristled at his impertinence. Somehow, though, she didn't feel as if she'd just met Hunter.

"My mother was a big fan of Edgar Allan Poe," she said, and waited to see if he'd get it.

He did, in record time. "'Once upon a midnight dreary, while I pondered, weak and weary, Over many a quaint and curious volume of forgotten lore...'" His voice took on a hushed urgency. "'Suddenly there came a tapping.'"

"You skipped part."

"'As of someone gently rapping.'" His knuckles thumped the table. "'Rapping at my chamber door.' Uh, something, something... 'Quoth the raven—'"

The three of them finished in unison: "'Nevermore.'"

Brent said, "Isn't there a Lenore in that poem? 'The lost Lenore?' Why didn't your mother name you after her?"

"My older sister beat me to that one. I'm not complaining."

Hunter's gaze lit on her hair, her eyes, her mouth. "I'm surprised she didn't name you Annabel." He said it quietly, his deep, mellifluous voice wrapping itself around the name in a way that raised gooseflesh all over her. In the mellow light of the club, she struggled to divine the color of his eyes. Blue or brown? They seemed to change with each breath.

Brent said, "Annabel? Now you've lost me."

Raven swallowed hard and dragged her attention back to her date. "'Annabel Lee.' Another of Poe's poems." A heartbreaking love poem.

Hunter shoved his hands in the pockets of his faded jeans, looking suddenly ill at ease. He seemed almost relieved when the waitress materialized with the appetizer assortment Brent had ordered. "Lisa," he told her, "no check for this table. It's on the house."

"I could pretend to argue with you," Brent said as he offered Raven the serving tongs, "or we could just skip over that part."

Hunter's grin was back in place as he told Raven, "Keep that cattle prod handy."

Then he was gone.

Brent launched into a lively discussion of Raven's work, asking how she'd come to be a hypnotherapist, what kind of training she'd received, what kind of problems she saw, proving that he wasn't the kind of self-absorbed male who only wanted to talk about himself. Raven found that gratifying, but it didn't help her concentrate on the conversation.

Brent hadn't noticed. Thank God. He'd been blessedly oblivious to what had been happening between his date and his brother.

And what exactly *had* been happening between his date and his brother? she asked herself. The proverbial once-in-a-lifetime meeting of soul mates? Or simple sexual awareness?

As if sexual awareness, once acknowledged, could ever be simple. Whatever it was, it hadn't been one-sided, that was for certain. Hunter had felt it, too. And it had made him as uncomfortable as it had made her.

With good reason, she thought, as she listened to the man her friends had chosen as suitable husband material praise her entrepreneurial initiative and order another Bass ale. Brent was a great guy, if first impressions were worth anything. She was committed to seeing him exclusively for three months, provided he was interested, and from the way he looked at her, the things he said, she was pretty sure he was interested.

Lord knew, she'd never willingly come between brothers by encouraging the attentions of one while dating the other. And if she read Hunter accurately, he wouldn't be party to something like that, either.

The meal progressed uneventfully. The club lights dimmed and the stage lights sprang on just as their dessert dishes were being cleared. Hunter leaped onto the stage and grabbed the mike off the stand.

Something banged inside Raven's chest.

Damn! she thought. *Why can't anything be simple?*

Hunter welcomed the audience to Stitches and threw out a couple of one-liners to get them primed. He was so relaxed up there that even when his second gag bombed, he made a joke about *that*. Raven watched in awe, partly because she'd never in her life be able to do what Hunter was doing, and partly because there he was, standing a few feet away, on a stage, under bright lights, and she could look at him all she wanted.

She was *supposed* to look at him. It would have been considered rude *not* to look at him! Greedily she followed every sexy, loose-limbed movement as he worked the crowd, drank her fill of that sheets-and-champagne voice.

"We have a special guest in the audience tonight," Hunter announced, prompting her to turn and scan the darkened club for a celebrity face. "The one and only Annabel Muldoon!"

Raven's head snapped around as a spotlight found her. She heard a few dubious responses—"Annabel who?"—and more than a few gasps of recognition, which should have struck her as hilarious. Brent obviously found the whole thing funny as hell; he was making a conspicuous effort not to crack up.

And everyone stared.

Hunter beckoned her onstage. "Come on up and say hi to your fans, Annabel! How about it, folks? Let's get Annabel Muldoon up here!"

The crowd by this time had decided Raven was Somebody, and responded with thunderous applause, punctuated by whoops and whistles of encouragement.

It was her worst nightmare.

Raven was breathing fast, trembling all over. Her hands were numb, rubbery lumps in her lap. She knew if she attempted to stand, her legs would never hold her. All she could manage was a little head shake.

Brent gave her a friendly shove. "Go on," he chuckled. "The crowd's going crazy. Have some fun."

"Come on, Annabel, don't be shy!" Hunter said, standing on the edge of the stage now, not eight feet away.

She looked up at him, struggling to govern her expression, praying that her misery wasn't there on her face for all to see. She wanted to say something, anything that might put an end to this torture, but her mind had seized up, and her tongue along with it.

Hunter's grin faltered for a fleeting instant as he stared at her. He backed away, signaling to the stagehand working the lights. The spotlight blinked off.

"Oh well, you know how skittish celebs are," Hunter told the audience, who sent up a collective groan of disappointment. Someone booed. "Next time I'll go through her agent. Now let's have a big hand for Richie Finley."

The crowd complied, and Hunter relinquished the stage to a massively obese man in an argyle sweater and corduroy slacks. "My name is Richard Finley," he began, deadpan, "but most folks call me Big Dick." One patron in back chortled at this lame opener.

Raven's panic attack began to subside. She rubbed warmth back into her hands and concentrated on breathing slowly through her nose.

Onstage, Finley plodded through his act. The audience wasn't very responsive, even when he got off one or two good lines, and Raven felt a stab of pity mixed with sheer awe at his audaciousness. Where, she wondered, did he find the courage? What wellspring of self-confidence allowed this man to walk out onstage under the glare of the spotlight and open his mouth?

Finley was followed by a black comedienne about Raven's age, whose routine focused on growing up in her dysfunctional extended family. She fared better than her predecessor, thanks to flawless timing and eloquent facial expressions. By the time she gave a little wave and walked off the stage, the audience was howling for more.

As a therapist, Raven was impressed by the way this woman had taken a painful episode in her life—her wretched upbringing—and turned it into something positive. It was as much a healing process as what Raven's phobia clients experienced when she helped them face their fears and learn to control them.

Raven hoped her clients never found out what a hypocrite she was. She knew she'd never find the inner fortitude to confront her own crippling fear. Tonight was just one more reminder of her failure, and a particularly humiliating one at that.

The audience laughed uproariously at everything uttered by the third and final comic, a grizzled middle-aged guy with a foul mouth and a sack of dopey props. He was funny, but he wasn't *that* funny. It slowly dawned on Raven that there were advantages to performing last. The audience had been loosened up by the first two acts and, most especially, by the liquor they'd consumed.

Several times patrons had approached her table,

shoving paper and pen under her nose, requesting an autograph, much to Brent's amusement. "My girl-friend's a big fan of yours," they'd say, or "I saw you on Letterman. When did you get out of rehab?" Raven had found the easiest course was to simply give them what they wanted, and by the end of the evening, she'd turned "Annabel" into a distinctive, flowing signature.

After the show, Brent excused himself to visit the men's room. Within seconds, Hunter materialized in the vacated seat, making her wonder if he'd been wait-ing to catch her alone.

She'd hoped she wouldn't have to face him. He knew. She'd seen it in his eyes, for that scant breath of time before he literally took her out of the spotlight.

Before she could think of some way to make light of the incident, he looked her straight in the eye and said, "I'm sorry."

She took a deep breath. "Let's not have this conver-sation."

Hunter leaned forward, folding his arms on the table. He looked down a moment, then back up at her, search-ing her eyes. "Raven. If I'd had an inkling that would make you uncomfortable, I never would've—"

"I know." She felt her composure slipping.

"I figured, after all that kidding around we did..."

"But that was just you and me." She twisted the nap-kin in her lap.

"Well, I really thought you'd enjoy getting up there and goofing around—a little Sonny and Cher stuff. You're funny. And quick with a comeback."

"This is just...something I've always had a problem with."

When she didn't elaborate, he said, "Performing in front of a crowd?"

"Well, public speaking. I've never even considered the idea of performing."

He cocked his head, giving her a speculative look. "You should, you know. You're a natural."

Despite everything, that preposterous statement drew a chuckle from her. "Not in this lifetime."

"Now you've done it. I can't resist a challenge."

The slow grin that accompanied this statement brought a return of those shivery goose bumps. Then the grin faded and he said quietly, "I really am sorry. It was presumptuous of me."

"Yeah, it was." She flashed a reassuring smile. "But no lasting damage was done. And anyway, it just reinforced what I already know—I have work to do."

"On what?"

"On myself. It's high time I learned to deal with this problem. Lalophobia, it's called. Fear of public speaking. I can't even give informal presentations, or talk to schoolkids on career day."

"What do you do?"

"I'm a hypnotherapist."

Hunter blinked. "No kidding."

"Not as much fun as a comedy club, but it's personally rewarding and it pays the bills." Raven scanned the club, looking for Brent.

Watching her, Hunter leaned back in his chair. "If

you're serious about working on your public speaking, every Wednesday is open-mike night here."

"Open mike?"

"Amateur night. Anyone can go up onstage and play stand-up comic."

"Thanks, but I don't think I'm ready for the major leagues. I think I'll start with something easier—like the State of the Union Address."

He came to his feet. "Well, you have an open invitation, if you change your mind."

Suddenly Brent was there. "An open invitation for what? What are you doing, making time with my date behind my back?" he joked.

"I'm trying to persuade Raven to work up some material for open-mike night."

"Great idea," Brent said, apparently oblivious to her earlier panic attack. "Listen, Raven, you ever go cross-country skiing?"

"Yes, as a matter of fact. I have skis and boots, but I haven't had a chance to use them so far this winter."

"There's this beautiful wooded park where I love to ski. I'm going out there on Sunday. You interested?"

"Sure, I'd love to."

"Why don't you join us, Hunter? Bring a date. After, maybe we can catch some dinner."

Bring a date. From which she deduced that Hunter had no steady girlfriend. Raven cursed the glimmer of satisfaction she felt. She had no business thinking of him that way.

Hunter's eyes flicked to Raven; she looked away

quickly. "I guess so," he said, "if it doesn't get too late. I have to open the club Sunday evening."

Brent asked, "Don't you have someone who can do that for you?"

"Uh, yeah, maybe," Hunter said, and Raven suspected he was as conflicted about this double date as she was.

"What the hell, I'll let Matt open up on Sunday." He smiled at her. "What's the worst that can happen?"

2

HUNTER WATCHED his show-off of a brother put even more distance between them as his skis streaked over the snow. That was what came of having your weekends free, he supposed—you got to be good at stuff that had nothing to do with booking comedians and supervising help and teetering on that scary tightrope between black ink and red. Hunter wouldn't trade Stitches for anything, but sometimes he envied Brent his job at that children's magazine, *Grasshopper*, and the regular paycheck that went with it.

The envy didn't stop there, he thought, glancing over his shoulder as Raven slid to a stop next to him. She was a graceful, competent skier, but not particularly fast. She'd unzipped her yellow down anorak halfway, revealing a black silk turtleneck tucked into faded jeans. She'd twisted that beautiful honey-colored hair back into a clip, but plenty of it was left loose to tumble around her face.

She smiled, breathing fast, her cheeks rosy from cold and exertion. It was a clear day, the late morning sun high in the sky, turning her pale brown eyes to burnished gold. Her hair and eyes were practically the same color, he noted. A twenty-four-karat lady.

Yesterday's snowstorm had dumped a good six inches on top of the previous accumulation, and they were breaking trail through white-clad trees and the occasional wide-open clearing. The light had that winter-pure clarity, and the air was sharp and cleansing. Hunter was glad he'd come.

"Brent is quite a skier," Raven said, peering through the trees. "I've lost sight of him already."

"You're not bad yourself."

"Oh, I'm slow. I'm holding everyone up."

Kirsten had turned back to rejoin them. "You're not holding anyone up, Raven. This isn't a race."

Despite her kind words, Hunter knew Kirsten was champing at the bit. A natural athlete, she'd learned to ski—both downhill and cross-country—at the age of three. As Hunter's date, she no doubt considered it rude to leave him in the dust, though Brent apparently suffered no such qualms where Raven was concerned. In fact, Kirsten couldn't have left Hunter in the dust if he didn't want to be left; he was a stronger skier than she. But somebody had to stay with Raven. That was what he told himself to justify his next words.

"Listen, Kirsten, there's no need for you to hold back. Why don't you catch up to Brent? We'll be along."

She hesitated, glancing at the tracks left by Brent's skis, as restless as a racehorse at the starting gate.

"Go on," he urged. "I know Brent thinks no woman can keep up with him."

That did it. Kirsten's eyes narrowed dangerously. A quick wave and she was gone.

"You should go on ahead, too," Raven said.

"No way, I need to catch my breath," he lied. "Looks like we're stuck with each other."

She glanced at him, then away. She'd done that a few times. Clearly he made her nervous, and he suspected he knew the reason for it. He *hoped* he knew the reason for it, which was pure idiocy on his part. He should have been hoping the attraction was one-sided, that she only had eyes for his brother.

His *brother*, he reminded himself, as he had about a hundred times since Friday night when he'd met her. Family loyalty was high on his list of personal values, a deeply ingrained part of him. You don't mess around with family loyalty.

Which means you don't even *think* about messing around with your brother's woman.

Not that she was Brent's woman, per se. Not yet. This was only their second date, but that made no difference. She was off-limits. End of discussion.

Which didn't stop him from wondering what had happened when Brent dropped her off at her home Friday night. Had she invited him in? Had they ended up in bed? He could ask Brent, but he didn't think he wanted to hear the answer.

Hunter planted his ski poles in the snow, shrugged off his backpack and set it at his feet. He pulled out a thermos. "I came prepared."

"Coffee?"

"Better." He uncapped the thermos and held it under her nose. Those gilded eyes widened in delight.

"Hot chocolate!"

Hunter poured some into the plastic thermos lid that doubled as a cup and handed it to Raven. She wrapped her gloved fingers around the steaming cup, brought it to her lips and sipped. She moaned, very faintly. Her eyes drifted closed, her expression one of rapture.

"More?" he asked when she handed the cup back. She shook her head and thanked him, said it really hit the spot. A little was left, and she watched as he tipped back the cup and finished it.

"Your eyes," she said, staring.

He smiled, pouring more cocoa. "A freak of nature."

"One blue and one brown." She gave a little laugh. "Like God couldn't make up his mind."

Hunter spread his arms. "A work in progress."

Raven opened her mouth to say something, and stopped. He wondered if she'd been about to comment on the state of the "work in progress." Instead she said, "Kirsten's nice."

"Yeah, she is. I met her on a wine-tasting tour of the North Fork vineyards." He drained the cup.

"Oh, yeah? Whose ID did she borrow?"

Chuckling with a mouthful of hot chocolate was a risky proposition. He managed to swallow and said, "Yeah, yeah, I know." He thought of the first impression Kirsten must have made on Raven, with those perky chestnut braids and that high, girlish voice and that wholesome, fresh-scrubbed face. Jail bait on skis. "But she's only five years younger than me."

"So that would make you what? Eighteen?"

"Ah, to be eighteen again. Try twenty-six."

Something flickered in her eyes, surprise or dismay, perhaps a mixture of both.

"I'm the baby of the family," he said, recapping the thermos and returning it to the backpack. "Brent's the oldest, followed by our sister, Tina. Poor old gal turned thirty a couple of years ago, and we have to listen to her whine and carry on about being a dried-up old maid."

This statement was met with stony silence.

"Her words, not mine," he swore, holding up a hand. "Scout's honor."

"Well, it's terrible that our youth-oriented society makes women so hung up about age. I'm sure Tina's a more interesting person now than when she turned twenty. She should be proud to be in her thirties."

"Well, maybe when she's had seven or eight years to get used to it like you have..."

Hunter savored Raven's bug-eyed outrage for a few moments before he cocked his finger at her and said, "Gotcha."

She made a wry face.

He asked, "What happened to all that thirty-something pride?"

"I'm working on it," she muttered.

"How long have you been working on it?"

"You get no points for subtlety, Hunter, but I'll tell you anyway. I turned thirty on Wednesday. January 7."

"Happy birthday. But really. I thought you were around my age."

"I choose to believe that particular fib. So much for renouncing society's hang-ups."

Hunter hefted the backpack and swung it onto one

shoulder. "Some guys only go for the real young girls. It boosts their egos or something, I guess. I'm not that way myself." Quickly he added, "And neither is Brent. You don't have to worry that he's going to think you're too, uh... What I mean is, he likes all kinds of women. A wide variety."

One eyebrow lifted. "How wide a variety?"

"Okay, I know how that sounded." *Like the truth.* "I just meant he's not picky, that's all."

There went the other eyebrow.

Hunter dropped his head back, groaning and chuckling at the same time. And to think he used to consider himself articulate. Then he caught her smirk, and asked, "You're enjoying this, aren't you?"

"Payback for those seven or eight years."

"There's no question my brother has very high standards in women." He tipped his head toward Raven; she rolled her eyes at the blatant flattery. "I only meant he's not one of those guys I was talking about."

"I know what you meant," she said with a reassuring smile, then hesitated. "As long as you're being so forthcoming about Brent, perhaps you don't mind telling me... My friend Amanda, who he works for, said Brent's been making noises like he wants to settle down. Would you say that's accurate?"

Hunter tried to imagine Raven Muldoon as his sister-in-law. He'd imagined her in a host of other roles since Friday night, in numerous scenarios involving a variety of exotic settings and more than a few intriguing positions.

But sister-in-law? That was one he couldn't quite bring into focus.

"It's accurate." He cleared his throat, struggling to banish the images he'd conjured. "Brent's set his sights on finding Mrs. Right. It's not just women who start thinking about things like that when they get to be a certain age."

"Just curious." She was blushing now. "I shouldn't have asked."

He shrugged. "We're not talking about a state secret here. He'd probably come right out and tell you himself if you asked him."

"Well, I couldn't really do that, but it wasn't fair to pump you for information."

Raven must feel pretty strongly about Brent, Hunter knew, if she was already thinking along these lines. Which made it all the more likely that Friday night's date had ended Saturday morning over French toast and latte.

"As for myself," he said, sliding his other arm through the backpack's strap and joggling it into place, "marriage is like world peace. It could happen, in theory, but I wouldn't wager any serious money on it."

"You never want to get married?"

"What I want is to get Stitches solidly in the black, book some impressive talent, establish it as the premier club on the Island. That's my priority, the commitment I made when I started it two years ago. It'll take a few more years, and it's all the responsibility I can handle at one time."

"Well, you're young," she said, zipping her jacket closed. "You have time."

"So do you."

She looked at him.

"I mean, you don't have to be in any hurry, Raven. The important thing is to make sure it's the right guy. Thirty's not exactly over the hill."

She said nothing, just snugged her jacket's stand-up collar around her throat.

"The temperature's dropping." He patted his backpack where the thermos was. "Do you want more—"

"No. We'd better catch up to the others. They'll be sending the Sherpas after us before long."

He started off, with her close behind. "I prefer a Saint Bernard with a cask of rum."

"Not amontillado sherry?"

He glanced over his shoulder to see her impish smile at this reference to Edgar Allen Poe's "The Cask of Amontillado." He charged ahead, propelling himself over the snow, hollering another of Poe's works at the top of his lungs.

"'It was many and many a year ago, In a kingdom by the sea...'"

Raven's spontaneous laughter warmed him from the inside out. "Don't tell me you memorized the whole thing!"

Grinning, he bellowed louder. "'That a maiden there lived whom you may know, By the name of Annabel Lee....'"

3

"ARE YOU SURE I can't help?" Raven asked from the doorway of Brent's kitchen. As soon as they'd arrived at his cozy ranch-style house on Long Island's North Shore, he'd started preparing dinner.

"Everything's under control." Brent smiled at her over his shoulder as he stirred something in a big pot on the stove. "Did you try that merlot?"

She lifted her wineglass. "It's wonderful. What are you making? It smells incredible."

"Jambalaya. What you smell is Cajun-style andouille sausage. I'm going to add shrimp at the end. Unless you're allergic to shellfish?"

"No, I love it."

"Great. Just relax. It'll be ready in about a half hour."

Brent looked completely at home in the kitchen, as confident and capable whipping up a batch of jambalaya as he was breaking trail through snow-covered woods. He was as genial and outgoing as he was self-assured. Raven had to admit she found the combination appealing, even sexy.

So why wasn't that special feeling bopping her over the head right about now? Her heart should be racing, she should be feeling light-headed, even a bit tongue-tied.

Perhaps it was the artificial nature of this arrangement, being set up by her matchmaking friends, that kept the giddy excitement at bay. It wasn't as if their nascent relationship were based on any kind of spontaneous animal magnetism.

Still, Raven was mature enough, experienced enough, to know that deep feelings didn't happen overnight. Superficial attraction might bop you over the head; true love took time and tender nurturing.

If she hadn't experienced that spontaneous animal magnetism with Brent's kid brother, there would be no problem. It was a purely physical response, she knew—and fleeting, she could only hope.

Unlike Hunter, Brent had marriage on the brain. Raven should be pleased, considering how skittish many men were when it came to commitment. However, earlier in the day, when she'd asked Hunter to verify that his brother was indeed in the market for a wife, she'd done so because her gut was warning her not to let Brent get too serious, too fast. Somehow she sensed he might not be as right for her as her friends assumed. The last thing she wanted was to lead him on, only to dash his hopes later.

Raven was obligated to date Brent for three months. She could afford to put on the brakes and slow things down, to see how compatible they were before going further.

She backed out of the kitchen, saying, "Well, let me know if I can do anything."

She entered the living room, which was comfortably furnished in shades of brown and brick-red, with blond wood accents. Kirsten sat on the love seat. She'd unbraided her hair, which now rippled around her face in shiny chestnut waves. If anything, she looked even younger than before, closer to sixteen than the twenty-one Hunter claimed.

Even twenty-one was a far cry from the big three-oh.

Thirty. Raven groaned inwardly. How had she let *that* happen?

Hunter sat on the floor between Kirsten's jeans-clad legs, leaning back against the love seat as she rubbed his shoulders, wide and thickly muscled under his wheat-colored sweater.

Hunter's eyes were closed, but they snapped open when Raven said, "Your brother's in there slaving away. He won't let me help." She settled into a blond rattan armchair.

"Don't tell me you're complaining," Hunter said with a smile.

"I can't believe he has any energy left after today. I'm whipped."

Kirsten said, "And I'm starved. Brent!" she called out. "Feed me before I collapse from hunger!"

From the kitchen Brent yelled, "So set the table if you're in such a hurry."

Laughing, Kirsten rose, swinging her lean leg over

Hunter's head. "He has no qualms about putting *me* to work!" She disappeared into the kitchen.

Alone with Hunter, Raven fiddled with her wineglass. The silence was thick and uncomfortable, until Hunter finally broke it.

"Brent's a terrific cook."

"I can tell," she said. "He's not even using a recipe."

Hunter glanced toward the closed door of the kitchen, through which they heard Kirsten and Brent's lively banter. Was he wishing his date would return? Was it possible he felt as ill at ease as Raven?

She brought the wineglass to her lips and took a fortifying gulp. Kirsten barreled out of the kitchen with a stack of plates and flatware, which she deposited on the table in the dining alcove.

Hunter straightened. "I'll help you."

Kirsten waved him away. "Relax. I've got this."

They watched her set the table, every movement as bouncy and energetic as if she'd spent the day lazing around the house. Raven, on the other hand, was stiff and sore from their hours of skiing. Compared to Kirsten, nearly a decade her junior, she felt like a withered crone.

Hunter's voice broke into her thoughts. "So. What makes hypnotherapy so personally rewarding?" At her quizzical expression, he said, "That's how you described it on Friday."

She saw something in his eyes that she hadn't seen in Brent's when he'd asked about her work. For Hunter, the question was more than polite chitchat; he really wanted to know.

She shrugged. "I like helping people. It's as simple as that. Not that all the cases are serious. Some people just want to concentrate better on sports or improve their study habits, that sort of thing. But most come to me with problems that severely affect their health, their ability to make a living, their quality of life. In many cases they've exhausted all conventional remedies."

"Do you get people who just can't be put under?"

"Not really. I get people who are nervous, who are under the typical misconceptions about hypnosis—that it's some kind of weird altered state, that the hypnotist can make them do things they don't want to do, stuff like that. First I have to earn their trust, make them comfortable enough to let down their guard and totally relax. That's all hypnosis is, really, a state of deep relaxation when you're more susceptible to suggestion."

His perceptive gaze seemed to reach deep within. "I bet you're good at that—putting people at ease. You have a gentle way about you. I can't imagine you willingly hurting another person."

There was a warm intimacy in his voice that both thrilled and unnerved her. Raven's fingers trembled as she set down her wineglass. "There must be something I can do for Brent."

She fled into the kitchen, where she made herself useful slicing Italian bread and making a Caesar salad. The meal lived up to her expectations. The jambalaya was a heavenly blend of rice, vegetables, shrimp and spicy sausage. The conversation was cheerful and animated. Though she knew it was premature, Raven imagined herself married to Brent, sharing his house, his kitchen, his bed. His brother.

Hunter would be her brother by extension—her brother-in-law. Part of her family. She sneaked a glance at him, only to find his eyes on her.

Oh, brother.

"WE CAN GIVE RAVEN a ride," Hunter offered, as he zipped up his black ski parka.

Raven sat next to Brent on the sofa. His arm was draped over her shoulders. Their dessert dishes and espresso cups littered the coffee table.

"Thanks anyway," Brent said. "I can drive her home later."

Raven looked at her watch, surprised to see it was after 1:00 a.m. "I have an early client tomorrow. I really should get going." Brent was disappointed, she could tell, but he yielded gracefully.

"Well, in that case, I'll let Hunter give you a lift." He rose and offered his hand. "Let's go find your jacket."

As if it needed finding. It was right there on Brent's bed, where he'd tossed it earlier. Raven wasn't surprised when he closed the door to his bedroom. They hadn't had a private moment all day. His smile was frank and affectionate as he approached her.

"I hope you've had as great a time as I have today," he said.

"I have, Brent. Thanks. Although..." She rotated her

shoulders, groaning and chuckling at the same time. "I may not be thanking you tomorrow. Maybe I should take a hot bath when I get home."

He cupped her shoulders and massaged them. His smile turned slightly devilish. "I've got a bathtub."

Raven knew he was offering more than a bath. She knew that if she didn't get in Hunter's car now, she wouldn't go home until the morning.

She couldn't claim she wasn't tempted. Despite her resolve to take things slow, Brent was a very attractive man. He was smart, attentive and obviously interested in her on more than a physical level. And it had been a long time since Raven had had sex. Of course, she'd never had sex this early in a relationship, but that wasn't the most compelling reason to say good-night now. The most compelling reason was waiting for her in the living room, jangling his car keys.

This whole thing was too confusing. Her gut told her that if she acted on impulse now, she'd live to regret it.

Brent leaned forward and touched his lips to hers. "A very comfortable bathtub," he murmured, and kissed her again, more firmly. "It fits two."

His technique wasn't bad. Direct without being obnoxious. She smiled to soften the blow. "Even if I didn't have the early appointment, I couldn't," she said. "I wouldn't."

He gave her a resigned smile. "I respect that."

When she emerged from Brent's bedroom moments later, Hunter's eyes lit on the jacket she carried. Perhaps he'd expected her to decline his offer after having spent two minutes alone with his brother.

Kirsten urged Raven to take the front passenger seat of Hunter's dark green Subaru Outback, since Kirsten would be dropped off first. Traffic was light, the roads clear and they chatted about the latest political scandal for the twenty minutes it took to get to Kirsten's apartment building.

Raven waited as Hunter collected Kirsten's ski gear from the trunk and walked her to the front door. It was clear he intended to escort her directly to her apartment door, but Kirsten kissed him soundly, grabbed her skis and gear bag, and shooed him back to the car and his waiting passenger. Hunter stood by the driver's door, waiting until lights shone in Kirsten's third-floor windows, before he slid behind the wheel and pulled out.

He continued their political discussion, and Raven was more than happy to have something to take her mind off things it had absolutely no business being on. By the time he pulled into the driveway of her home, they'd exhausted current events and were starting in on the weather.

"This is a pretty big place for one person," Hunter said, as he eyed the big split-level house. "Do you have roommates?"

"No, it's just me." Raven accompanied him to the rear of the Outback, where he opened the trunk and slid out her skis and gear bag. "This was my parents' home. My sister, Lenore, and I grew up here. Mom and Dad sold it to me—at very favorable terms, need I add—

when they retired to Florida a few years ago. It is a little bit too much house for me, but it has a feature I need—a separate entrance for my business." She nodded toward the side door leading to her hypnotherapy office.

Hunter insisted on carrying her skis to the house. Raven unlocked the front door and tried to relieve him of his burden, but he sidestepped her and crossed the threshold into the vestibule. "Where do these go?"

"Oh, you can leave them right here. I'll put them away later."

He hesitated before placing the bag on the floor and leaning the skis against the wall. Raven had switched on the overhead lamp, casting his features in a harsh landscape of light and shadow.

"Thanks so much for the ride, Hunter."

He nodded stiffly. "My pleasure." After an awkward moment he said, "Well, good night." He started to leave, but turned back in the next breath. "You know, I think you could help me."

"What?"

He rubbed his jaw, bristly with the day's growth of whiskers. "The more I think about it, well, hypnosis might be just what I need."

"Oh. What do you need help with?"

"Fear of heights. I get, you know, real anxious in high places. Panicky. Do you handle that kind of problem?"

"Of course," she said. "I've helped several clients with acrophobia."

"Great. That's great. We'll do that, then. When?"

"Um...I'll have to check my calendar. Why don't you

call me tomorrow afternoon—I mean this afternoon—
and we'll set up a time."

Hunter grinned. "I'll do that. What's your number?"

Raven produced a business card from her purse.

He asked, "Think you can fit me in this week?"

"I'm pretty sure I have a couple of openings."

Hunter studied the card. "Listen, Raven, you won't
mention this to Brent, will you?"

"Not if you don't want me to."

"It's just, uh, a little embarrassing, you know? He
doesn't even know I have this hang-up. I'd rather we
kept it between us."

"No problem."

"Thanks." He offered a jaunty salute with the card
and let himself out of the house.

4

"YOU SEEM A LITTLE nervous," Raven said. "That's perfectly natural the first time."

It wasn't apprehension over being hypnotized that had Hunter on edge. During the half week he'd waited for his 10:00 a.m. Thursday appointment, all he'd thought about was seeing Raven again. The thrill of anticipation had warred with guilt over the blatant lie he'd concocted for no more worthy purpose than to steal some time alone with his brother's girlfriend.

Fear of heights. It was the first thing that had popped into his head.

"Have a seat here." Raven gestured toward a brown leather recliner. They were in her office, a cozy room paneled in oak and decorated in earth tones. With the exception of the recliner, all of the furniture appeared to be antique. A massive rolltop desk stood against one wall, flanked by glass-fronted bookcases.

Raven had drawn heavy drapes over the windows, blocking out the dismal gray winter sky. An amber-colored, stained-glass floor lamp spread its toasty glow throughout the room. The two of them were sequestered in this snug, inviting space for the next hour, cocooned against the outside world. It was easy to see how an intimate setting such as this could promote the sharing of one's deepest thoughts, fears and desires.

Perhaps, Hunter reflected, as Raven pulled a rocking chair close to his recliner and sat in it, this wasn't such a great idea, after all. He began to wonder if he'd gotten in over his head. She was close enough that he could detect the scent she wore, a fresh, powdery fragrance—innocent and alluring at the same time. She wore a soft-looking beige turtleneck sweater, belted over a calf-length paisley skirt. Her feet were encased in brown suede half boots.

Hunter leaned the recliner back into its flattest position. He linked his hands over his middle, then moved them to the armrests, before returning them to his waist. He squirmed. He sighed. "There. I'm comfortable," he announced. "Totally relaxed."

She chuckled. "If you say so. Don't worry about it. You will be soon enough. Do you have any questions before we start?"

She was leaning a little to one side in the rocker, with her legs crossed, idly tapping her pen on the small notebook on her lap. The warm lamp glow picked out glittering highlights in her hair. She looked lovely and serene and totally trusting. Hunter felt like a heel.

He asked, "Will I remember what we talk about?"

"Probably. As I said before, hypnosis is simply a state of relaxation. It can be as light as when you're engrossed in a movie or a good book—or as deep as the brink of sleep. Most people remember everything that happens, because it usually isn't that deep."

Hunter had no intention of letting the "trance," or whatever it was called, get anywhere near that intense. He wasn't here to snooze.

"Okay, well..." He spread his hands. "Let's get down to it."

"First, I want you to close your eyes."

"Do I have to?" He was staring at her.

She smiled. "I'm the boss here. Close your eyes."

He did.

"I want you to think back to the most relaxing, soothing place you've ever experienced. It could be anywhere."

"That's easy. The beach. Just vegging out, soaking up the rays. It's my favorite place."

"Go there now, Hunter. Take yourself back to the last time you were at the beach. You're lying on a blanket—"

"Towel."

He heard the smile in her voice. "A towel. The sun is bright overhead, and hot, but not too hot. You've been in the water, and you can feel the droplets drying on your body."

Raven's voice was tranquil, evenly modulated. Hunter could listen to it for hours.

"The towel is soft and nubbly," she continued. "The sand underneath it conforms to your body perfectly. You hear the waves rolling up, as regular as clockwork. To you, it's always been the most soothing sound in the world."

How could she know that? The sun's brilliant glow

penetrated Hunter's closed eyelids. Waves rumbled ashore, foaming over the sand and receding in a timeless cadence. He breathed deeply, filling his lungs with the mingled perfumes of salt spray and the intoxicating essence that was Raven's alone.

"You feel the sun's heat on the top of your head," she said, "drying your hair, making your scalp tingle, making the underlying muscles relax completely as all the tension there evaporates with the water."

"Mmm-hmm," he grunted, as waves of tension wafted from his scalp to dissipate like fog under the hot summer sun.

Raven continued the process of physical relaxation, naming each part of him in turn, from his facial muscles on down. By the time she reached his toes, he was a formless sack of jelly, lying slack and boneless on his imaginary beach towel.

Raven's mellow voice centered Hunter. Her words registered on a deeper level, as if they were his own thoughts. Never before had he experienced this sense of connectedness with another person.

"I want you to think back to a time when you felt safe," Raven said. "Safe and secure and confident."

The first image to come to mind was a childhood memory of his family sitting around the dinner table. Family dinnertime was sacrosanct, the one point in their busy day when everyone got a chance to share, decompress, clown around.

Raven said, "When you feel safe and confident, nod your head."

Hunter gave a little nod.

"I'm going to touch your right hand," she said, and he felt her cool, delicate fingers on the back of his hand. In the next moment they were gone.

"Think back to another time when you felt the same way," Raven said, "safe and protected and self-assured."

Obediently Hunter delved into his memory banks, and again Raven touched his right hand. They repeated the process a few more times.

Raven said, "Now I want you to think back to an unpleasant experience you've had with heights. An incident that made you panicky, apprehensive."

She sounded so warmly sincere, so reassuring, Hunter felt immediately ashamed for his subterfuge. His mind obligingly provided him with a situation that had disconcerted him, though it had nothing to do with heights. He recalled last Friday night, in his club, Stitches, when his instant, animal attraction to his brother's date had whacked him over the head like a two-by-four.

Family loyalty, duty and honor were a cornerstone of his life, and he knew the same was true for Brent. It was the way they'd been raised. Brent would cut off his right arm before he'd come on to a woman Hunter was seeing. Not that the guy didn't have his faults. Hell, Hunter was no angel, either. But you only had one family.

What Hunter was doing was wrong. He vowed that after today, he'd stay the hell away from Raven.

She asked, "Are you feeling it now, Hunter? The dis-. comfort and anxiety? Nod if you are."

He emitted a ragged sigh. He nodded.

Her voice was heartbreakingly gentle. "This time I'm going to touch your left hand."

He felt the light pressure on his left hand. They repeated the exercise several times, Raven asking him to dredge up an unpleasant incident involving fear of heights, followed by the touch on his left hand. Each time his mind filled in the blanks by translating fear of heights into fear of becoming the kind of bottom-feeding bastard who would sneak around behind his brother's back, making time with his woman.

Again she instructed him to call up an uncomfortable memory, and again she said, "I'm going to touch your left hand." Only this time, she surprised him by touching his right hand instead.

"You're feeling the security and comfort you've come to associate with my touching your right hand," she explained, "even though you're thinking about an experience that caused you anxiety."

Hunter was astonished to realize it was true.

Several more times she asked him to recall negative height-related memories, and each time she touched his right hand. He found that when he received this "good" touch while thinking about what a snake he was, he didn't feel like such a snake, after all.

Hunter decided he liked not feeling like a snake. And had he really done anything so terrible? If Brent ever found out about this little charade, they'd probably have a good laugh together.

That thought brought him instantly awake.

The hell they would.

Blinking, he looked at Raven. She tipped her head, with a little smile. "You came out of that pretty fast," she said.

"I guess I'm just not used to this yet."

"Did anything I say disturb you?"

"No, I just..." *Tell her you're not coming back.* He looked at his watch. "Wow, our time's almost up."

She leaned forward, looked at him earnestly. "What we did today was only one technique for helping you to overcome your problem—we can explore others if you decide to continue the therapy. Do you feel like you've made progress?"

"Yes." *I've decided, Raven. I can't come back here.* He tried to make the words come as he tilted the recliner up, stood and prepared to leave.

Raven stood, too, leaving her notebook and pen on her chair. "Do you want to schedule another session?"

Say no. "Sure."

"Same time next week?"

"Why not?" He tugged his wallet out of his back pocket, extracted the check for her fee and handed it to her.

Hunter was definitely in over his head, and willingly digging himself in deeper as he said, "*Your* first therapy session is scheduled for next Wednesday, 9:00 p.m."

She looked delightfully baffled. "What's next Wednesday at nine?"

"Open-mike night at Stitches."

"Oh no!"

"Oh yes, Raven. You're going to overcome your fear of public speaking. You have work to do, remember? That's how you put it."

"I can't. I won't," she said, as she backed up, folding her arms across her chest. "It's out of the question."

Hunter laughed. "Raven, it's not that terrifying."

"For you, perhaps. Hunter, you saw me the other night, when you were inviting me up onstage. Don't tell me you don't know how much this whole thing wigs me out."

"I thought you were the expert on getting over things that wig you out."

Her mulish expression became more mulish. He'd hit a nerve.

"You help people overcome their phobias all the time," he said. "Shouldn't you be able to—"

"I don't want to talk about it."

"Raven." He closed the distance between them. She looked stunning in the golden lamplight, soft and vulnerable and much too kissable for his peace of mind. Hunter struggled to keep from touching her. God only knew where one touch would lead.

"Listen to me." He jammed his hands in his jeans pockets. "I know the idea terrifies you. But that's why you have to do it. To prove to yourself that you can. To gain control over this senseless fear that keeps you from giving professional presentations and talking to the schoolkids and all that."

"I know you mean well, but I just can't."

Her eyes pleaded with him. She was hugging herself. Clearly, even the thought of getting up on that stage made her weak in the knees. But Hunter discerned an inner strength in Raven that he doubted she recognized in herself. She had so much to offer—and so much to gain—if she could put a leash on this baseless phobia.

He took a step closer, until mere inches separated them. His gaze locked on to hers. "I'll be there," he said, quietly. "I'll be right there the whole time. I won't let anything bad happen to you, Raven."

For several dangerous, exhilarating moments, as he stared down into her wide, unblinking eyes, the two of them connected on a plane neither wanted to admit existed. The certainty of their mutual desire arced between them like electricity, until the very air seemed charged with it.

Raven dragged her gaze away first. She pulled in a deep breath. Hunter took a step back.

"You only have to come up with about three to five minutes of material," he said. "I put a lot of people on during open-mike night, sometimes a couple of dozen. You get up there, throw out a few lines, you're off the stage before you know it."

Raven made an exasperated sound. "I've seen amateur acts. The audience is really critical. I mean, you put a big name up there, the guy could read a shopping list and he'll get the laughs. Put a nobody like me onstage, it'll be like sharks scenting blood."

"Look, I'm not going to lie to you. It's rough going up there, especially the first couple of times. But nothing is gained in life if you don't take risks."

Raven had half turned away. Hunter leaned to one side to peek at her face. A surly glare was his reward.

"I'll let you practice your routine on me," he offered, "although I don't think you'll need much help. You're naturally funny, Raven. You have a good sense of timing. You cracked us all up at dinner the other night talking about your friend Sunny who's hooked on the home-shopping channels."

Her lips quirked in a reluctant smile. "Truth is stranger than fiction."

"That's exactly it. Work from real life. Embellish on your experiences. Just get up there and tell a story."

She made that funny sound again.

"And I'll tell you something. The reason I know you'll do great, the reason you're naturally funny, is the *way* you say things. It isn't what you say, it's the delivery. The timing. You have a gift for it."

"I'll think about it."

"You're just trying to placate me, and it won't work. I'm scheduling you for next Wednesday."

"No! Not yet. Let me—let me think about it."

That was what she said, but the undiluted panic on her face told him she'd crossed the threshold. She'd decided to do it.

Hunter lifted his dark green down vest from the antique coat rack and slipped it on over his frayed gray sweatshirt. "You won't regret it, Raven. Remember, I'll be right there with you. If they start pelting you with rotten fruit, I'll get the hook and yank you offstage."

She scowled. "That is so not funny."

Hunter grinned, high on the thrill of victory. "It'll be great, you'll see. When it's over, you'll wonder what you were so scared of." He grabbed her notebook from the rocker and jotted his phone number on the cardboard cover. "Work up some material, then give me a call and we'll get together to go over it."

On his way out the door, Hunter gave her a quick kiss on the cheek. "Think funny thoughts."

5

THE AIR WAS SO COLD Raven had to wrap a scarf around her lower face to warm her breath. A floppy black beret protected her ears. She was bundled up in a silk turtle-neck and heavy wool sweater under her yellow down anorak, but the cold cut through her jeans like a knife.

Still, it was exhilarating riding on horseback through the woods. This was her third date with Brent, and she was beginning to appreciate his preference for vigorous physical activity. Their fourth date was already sched-uled for next Saturday: ice-skating on a frozen lake, fol-lowed by a home-cooked meal at her house. The follow-ing day Brent was hosting a big Super Bowl party, and she'd promised to make a double batch of her fiery chili con carne for it.

He'd promised to teach her to play racquetball and, since he had a pilot's license, to take her flying over Manhattan. The rented airplane wouldn't be fancy, he warned, a "Volkswagen with wings," but Raven knew it would take the prize as Most Adventurous Date of her life.

She'd never ridden a horse before, although she was getting the hang of it, moving at a brisk gait between the trail guide in front and Brent behind her. She'd never played racquetball or flown in a private plane, either, but something told her she'd enjoy those experiences just as much. What a delight to go out with a man whose imagination wasn't limited to dinner and a movie.

"You're not used to this," Brent said. "How are your hindquarters holding up?"

She grinned at him over her shoulder. "That's a very personal question, don't you think?"

His cheeks were pink, his blue eyes glistening from the cold. His impish expression made him look younger, more like his brother. He was as handsome as Hunter, though in a different way. Brent's face was more mature, his hair always neatly trimmed, his wardrobe more put together than Hunter's. Today he wore a brown leather bomber jacket over an ivory wool turtleneck and snug, new-looking black jeans. His brown riding boots appeared freshly polished.

Brent, no novice to riding, sat his horse with confident ease, the reins held loosely in his gloved fingers. The stable had provided him with a big, dun-colored mare, somewhat more spirited than the small, placid chestnut that Raven rode.

He said, "Well, you'll be happy to know that from where I sit, your hindquarters are holding up just fine."

She laughed. Brent had a way of being flirtatious and even suggestive without making her uncomfortable. They'd gotten along well from the start. Perhaps Amanda had known what she was doing when she'd suggested setting Raven up with him. And perhaps

Charli and Sunny had known what they were doing when they'd rubber-stamped the choice. Raven knew Brent was probably on his best behavior, as people tended to be in the early stages of a relationship, but she had to believe that if he had any truly obnoxious qualities, they would have revealed themselves by now.

When they arrived back at the stables, Brent gallantly helped Raven dismount. She rubbed her mount's velvety nose and thanked her for putting up with a neophyte such as herself.

Brent put his arm around Raven as they walked to his red Acura. Holding the passenger door open for her, he checked his watch. "It's only a quarter to five. Plenty of time to make our seven-thirty reservation."

They planned to grab showers at Raven's house before heading out to an elegant dinner at the Island's newest five-star restaurant. Brent had packed a bag with fresh clothes to change into. It was nearly dark by the time they pulled into Raven's driveway. She invited him to make use of the master bathroom while she checked her answering machine and went through her mail.

Twenty minutes later, Raven was sitting in her office, answering e-mail at her computer, when she heard Brent descend the stairs.

"In here," she called.

Within moments, his clean, soapy scent teased her nostrils. His hands settled on her shoulders as he stood behind her. "This must be where you practice your unholy craft," he teased. "The sanctum sanctorum."

"This is it. I'll be finished here in a minute."

Brent's strong hands kneaded her shoulders. "You did very well for your first time riding. Are you sore?"

She chuckled. "Yeah, but not there."

His fingers slipped forward and massaged a bit lower, almost but not quite touching her breasts. Raven wanted to say, *Not there, either.*

Abruptly his hands stilled. "Is that Hunter's phone number? It is," he said as he lifted Raven's notebook from the desktop and examined the seven digits scrawled on the cover in his brother's distinctive handwriting.

Raven's heart slammed into her ribs. Her mind raced. She'd promised not to tell Brent about Hunter's hypnotherapy. This wasn't the first time a client had requested her to be discreet, but never before had discretion felt more like some kind of illicit secret.

She forced her voice to be steady. "I told you, he talked me into performing at Stitches on Wednesday. He gave me his number so we could go over my routine."

Brent tossed the notebook back onto the desk. "He was here?"

"Um, yes, when he dropped me off that night after skiing. He wanted to see my—" her chuckle was strained "—sanctum sanctorum." Why did that suddenly sound so dirty?

Thankfully, Brent seemed to accept this explanation. He bent over her. His wet hair tickled her ear. "You

know, we have plenty of time before we have to leave.''
He pressed a light kiss to her temple.

The intimate murmur sounded so much like Hunter's
voice that Raven felt a jolt of unease. She looked over
her shoulder and only then realized Brent's torso was
bare. *Please don't let him be wearing a towel,* she thought
as her gaze skipped lower.

He wore taupe dress slacks, she was relieved to see.

''Um, let me just send this.'' She pushed a few buttons
and her e-mail to her father in Fort Lauderdale zipped
out into cyberspace.

Brent spun her desk chair until she faced him. He
braced his palms on the armrests and leaned over her,
his smile provocative. In that instant Raven realized
their relationship had progressed past flirtatious banter—at least as far as Brent was concerned.

He touched his lips to hers. ''Plenty of time,'' he repeated, and kissed her again.

Brent was an accomplished kisser. The sensation was
pleasurable, but Raven found it impossible to relax and
enjoy it, wondering how far he intended to take this.
She didn't have to wonder for long.

''Come here,'' he said, pulling her to her feet and
steering her to the recliner—right where Hunter had sat
two days before. Brent sat and pulled her onto his lap.
Raven found herself snugged against his warm bare
chest.

''Brent...''

Suddenly he tilted the chair back so it was nearly hor-
izontal. She stiffened.

"I—I must smell like a horse," she said, doing a push-up over Brent, trying to keep from sprawling on top of him.

"Let me see." He nuzzled her throat. "Mmm...you don't smell like any horse I've ever met." He stroked her back coaxingly, exerting mild pressure, urging her to relax against him. "I like this chair." He wagged his eyebrows. "It has infinite possibilities."

"This is where my hypnotherapy clients sit." Raven tried in vain to lever herself off him.

"How fitting," Brent said. "I'm under your spell already."

"No, I mean...this isn't right. I'm not comfortable doing this here."

His gaze was frankly seductive. "Then let's go upstairs." He cupped his hand over her breast and caressed her.

Raven grasped his wrist. "No."

Brent froze. He removed his hand and pushed the chair upright.

Raven rose and took a wobbly step backward. "This is going too fast for me, Brent."

He sighed in frustration. "This is our third date."

"Is that some magic number?" She offered a wry smile, and was gratified when he returned it.

"I was hoping it would be."

"I can't...get intimate this soon. It's not my way." Raven wished he'd get up from the recliner. She couldn't see Brent sitting there without thinking about his brother.

"I can wait," he said, "but I need to know where you see this going. I'll be frank, Raven. I'm already pretty serious about you. I want to take it to the next level—and I'm not just talking about sex. You're a very special woman."

"I like you a lot, Brent. I'm really glad Amanda introduced us. I'm just not ready for more right now."

He studied her. "Can I assume there's no one else?"

"Of course there's no one else! I mean, I'm not the type to see more than one person at a time." She smiled. "Life's complicated enough."

The corners of his eyes crinkled. "Looks like I've gotten myself entangled with an old-fashioned girl."

"Let's just say I know what works for me."

"That's more than a lot of people can claim." Brent rose and pulled her lightly into his arms. "All right. We'll take things slow. Some things in life are worth the wait."

6

RAVEN GLANCED AROUND HER, scanning the crowd at Stitches. The place was packed to capacity: good news for Hunter, less than thrilling for Raven as she contemplated stepping out onstage in a short while. Whatever had possessed her to say yes?

But she knew the answer to that. In her mind's eye she saw Hunter as he'd looked in her office after his session last Thursday, saw the forthright sincerity in his eyes, heard it in his voice as he promised he wouldn't let anything bad happen to her.

She smiled. Her white knight, ready to slay the dragons for her.

The patrons had finished dinner and were now enjoying dessert. To her right, Charli sipped espresso and spooned up the last of her lemon sorbet. Amanda, sitting on Raven's left, had eschewed dessert in deference to her waistline and was nursing a cup of jasmine tea. Across the table, Sunny was working on her second cup of coffee as she polished off a jumbo helping of apple crisp à la mode.

Raven had sent her pizza rustica back untouched. Trying to force something into her stomach when she was this keyed up was a losing proposition.

"Get me out of here," she groaned, for the dozenth time.

And for the dozenth time, Charli placed a reassuring hand over hers. "You'll do great, Raven."

"You need a drink," Amanda said, "something to take the edge off."

"That's the last thing I need. I want to have all my faculties intact when I humiliate myself."

Amanda shrugged. "Suit yourself. If it was me going up on that stage, I'd have a pint of Johnnie Walker with a Thorazine chaser."

Sunny set down her fork. "That's really helpful, Amanda. She's nervous enough."

"Don't worry," Raven said. "Nothing can make this worse for me. How do I look?"

"Good news," Amanda said. "You look funny."

Charli tsked. "Amanda, will you stop? You look really nice, Raven. That green's a good color for you."

"Thanks." Raven plucked at the moss-green chenille sweater she'd paired with a floral calf-length skirt. "I figure when I throw up from nerves, it won't show so much on this."

"Do you mind?" Sunny said, with her mouth full. "Some of us are still eating."

"Guys, I really appreciate your being here for me," Raven said. "Now remember, laugh long, laugh hard, laugh often."

Hunter's voice broke in. "Instructing your shills?"

Raven looked up. He'd stopped at their table, standing between her and Charli. He laid a warm, heavy hand on Raven's shoulder. Did he have any idea how comforting that simple gesture was?

Amanda said, "You must be Brent's brother." Introductions were made around the table.

Hunter shook hands with Charli last. He smiled down at her. "What's Charli short for? Charlotte? Charlene?"

Even in the low light of the club, Raven saw her friend blush. Charli Rossi was unaccustomed to even this much attention from a man.

In a small voice she said, "Carlotta."

"That's a great name." He nodded toward her empty demitasse cup. "Something tells me you might be a good one to ask. How does our espresso rate, Carlotta?"

She smiled shyly. *"Delizioso."*

Amanda glanced at Sunny. If Raven didn't know them so well, she might not have caught the hidden meaning behind the subtle look they exchanged.

They couldn't be serious! Charli and Hunter?

Hunter said, "Where's Brent? I thought he'd be here."

"He couldn't make it," Raven said. "He has some kind of poker tournament tonight—it was scheduled months ago."

"Oh," was all Hunter said, but watching him, Raven sensed that Brent's absence didn't sit well with him. She resisted the urge to defend Brent. The fact was, it didn't sit well with her, either, but she had no right to object. They'd been dating less than two weeks—and wasn't she the one who wanted them to take things slow?

Hunter said, "Raven, I'm putting you on last. When you hear me introduce Donny Deaver, just come back-stage."

All she could manage was something between a groan and a sigh.

Hunter squeezed her shoulder. He didn't say anything. The gesture was more comforting than words could ever be.

After he left them, Amanda pounced on Charli. "'How does our espresso rate, *Carlotta?*'" She drew out the name in a throaty purr.

"Oh, stop!" Charli glanced around fretfully.

"Hunter seems like a real sweetheart," Sunny said, scraping her fork over her dessert plate. To Raven she said, "Is he as nice as his brother?"

"Well...I guess so. I mean, I haven't been around him much."

Sunny squeezed Charli's arm. "Something tells me we won't have to look far when it's time to find you a guy."

"Keep it in the family." Amanda winked. "Raven with Brent, Charli with Hunter."

"That's ridiculous!" Raven snapped.

The other three looked at her.

"I mean...Hunter's only twenty-six."

"A four-year difference." Sunny shrugged. "So what?"

"A younger man," Amanda said. "Yum."

Sunny smirked at Amanda. "There was a time when you got all excited over *older* men."

"Seriously." Amanda leaned toward Charli. "I think Hunter's interested. Do you like him?"

Before Charli could formulate an answer, Raven said, "I can't believe you guys! A few friendly words and you've practically got them married off!"

Charli stared wide-eyed at Raven. Amanda and Sunny shared another of those knowing looks, and Raven slid lower in her seat.

"Well, well, well." Amanda leaned back again, wearing a silky smile.

"Overreacting just a tad, aren't we, Raven?" Sunny offered.

Charli blinked at Raven. "You have a thing for Hunter?"

"God! Of course not! What's wrong with you people?"

Amanda laughed. "Yeah, right."

"Give it up, Raven." Sunny was grinning. "We've known you too long."

"It's not funny," Charli said. "She's supposed to be dating Brent."

"I *am* dating Brent! And only Brent!"

Amanda clutched her heart. "Ah, but you lust in your heart for his hunky little brother."

Now it was Raven's turn to glance nervously around. "It's not like that. Hunter's attractive—so what? Can't I find someone attractive without you guys blowing it out of proportion? And even if he weren't too young, he's off-limits because—" Raven bit her tongue.

"Because why?" Amanda demanded.

Because he's my hypnotherapy client, Raven thought, but she wouldn't violate his confidence by saying it. Getting involved with a client was a clear breach of ethics.

Raven sighed. "Look, can we just drop this?"

"What are you going to do about Brent?" Sunny asked.

Charli straightened. "She's going to keep seeing him for the full three months, like she agreed back when we set up the Wedding Ring."

"That's right," Raven said, knowing how much importance Charli placed on adhering to the pact they'd all made way back when.

"There was a reason we made that three-month rule," Charli continued, uncharacteristically assertive. "Raven says she doesn't like Hunter that way, and that's good enough for me." She held up her palm as Amanda started to interrupt. "And no, I'm not saying that because I want him for myself. He's a friendly guy. What do you think, that I'm so lonely, so desperate, that I'll turn a few kind words into a declaration of love?" Charli was flushed with indignation.

Amanda said quietly, "Of course not. That's not what I meant. I guess we're just kind of jumping the gun."

"Anyway, it's not my turn yet," Charli said, as the waitress removed their dirty dishes. "Let's concentrate on Raven."

Thankfully, the show started, quelling further discussion. Raven would be on last, Hunter had said. She wondered if he'd done that on purpose, recalling how much more receptive the audience was after they'd been warmed up. She'd met with him on Monday to go over her routine. He'd helped her streamline it, had given her tips and expressed enormous confidence in her.

Hunter came onstage and tossed out a few one-liners to rev up the crowd. The first act came on. Raven noticed little outside of the man's high, grating voice and the oversize fedora that practically hid his eyes. Panic threatened to suffocate her. The familiar symptoms were out in force: shallow breathing, clammy hands, a dry mouth that stayed that way no matter how many sips of water she took.

Act followed act, with each amateur performer remaining onstage up to five minutes. As short as each routine was, Raven had no doubt that for the person up there in the spotlight, it must seem like forever. She concentrated on regulating her breathing.

It wasn't working.

"Raven, go!" Charli urged. "He's bringing on that Donny guy."

Charli and Amanda patted her back as Raven woodenly rose and began to weave her way among the tables. Earlier she'd joked about throwing up from nerves, but at the moment it seemed an all-too-real possibility.

She made her way through a doorway and down a short hall to the narrow waiting area just off the stage, where a burly, unkempt guy with a huge, bushy beard was waiting his turn to go on. She offered a weak smile,

which he answered with a sneer. She watch Donny
Deaver in profile as he tossed out limp one-liners,
which were met with silence from the audience.

This guy was awful! Raven cringed, watching Donny
sweat under the lights, listening to him stumble over his
overrehearsed lines as the hum of audience chatter began to drown out his act.

Raven's legs felt like rubber bands. She sank into a
ratty metal folding chair that was wedged between
cases of beer and an empty janitor's bucket.

You can do this, she told herself, praying that once she
was actually out there, her memory wouldn't desert her
and she'd recall her routine.

She helped people overcome their phobias all the
time, as Hunter had reminded her. If she couldn't manage to get a grip on her own hang-ups, she was nothing
more than a fraud.

Raven closed her eyes. She took a deep, slow breath,
consciously blocking out Donny's voice, the impatient
murmur of the crowd. She pulled in another lungful of
air, feeling her tight chest begin to relax. She kept her
eyes closed, her hands resting in her lap.

Raven took herself to her own special place, the place
that always put her at ease. Silently she commanded
each part of her body in turn to go slack, willed her
heartbeat to slow its frantic pace. She concentrated on
increasing the blood flow to her extremities, and felt her
fingers warm fractionally.

Another deep breath, and another. When she felt as

centered and calm as possible under the circumstances, she opened her eyes and looked right into Hunter's.

He was squatting directly in front of her, his forearms on his knees. His smile was gentle and reassuring and something else, something she chose not to explore just then.

"Where were you?" he asked.

Despite everything, she returned his smile. "Where else? The beach."

The same place Hunter had chosen during his hypnotherapy session.

Donny had been replaced onstage by the bearded fellow, whose belligerent brand of humor wasn't going over well with the audience. His "comedy" routine seemed to consist of running down every woman he'd ever known, and had more to do with spite than wit.

The sick dread began to bubble to the surface once more. "Hunter," Raven whispered, "I really don't think I can do this."

His eyes never left hers as he took her hands in his and rubbed his thumbs over the backs. His fingers felt dry and startlingly hot. "Raven. Ask yourself, what's the worst that can happen?" He must have sensed she was thinking up a droll rejoinder, because he added, "Seriously."

She took a deep breath. "Seriously? I could make a serious ass of myself."

"You don't know those people out there. Except for your buddies, and they care about you, they love you. Who gives a damn what the rest of them think?"

Where did that leave Hunter? Was he one of "the rest of them," or did he see himself as one of her close friends, someone who cared about her, who—

Raven slammed the lid on that line of thought. "What you're saying is rational, but there's nothing rational about this lalophobia of mine. It's a gut-level thing."

"Listen. When you're out there, pretend you're talking to Amanda and Charli and Sunny. Just to them."

"I'll try," she said, but she doubted it would work. "You know, if it weren't for you, coaching me, giving me these pep talks and all, I wouldn't have the courage to do this."

"I thought you were going to say if it weren't for me, you wouldn't be suffering like this."

She gave a shaky chuckle. "That, too."

He squeezed her hands. She looked into those remarkable eyes of his, and felt that dangerous invisible net pull tighter around the two of them. Onstage, the woman-bashing would-be comic turned his insult humor on the audience as they started to heckle him.

She whimpered, "Please tell me I'm not next."

Hunter rose, pulling her up with him; he had to feel how badly she was shaking. "You're next."

She jerked her hands out of his grip. "Hunter, listen to them! It's a feeding frenzy out there!"

"Don't worry, I won't let them draw blood." With that he trotted onto the stage and deftly steered the performer off it. The man shoved past Raven, snarling something she was just as happy she couldn't make out.

"Our last act this evening is Raven Muldoon,"

Hunter announced. "This is Raven's first time onstage, so let's make her feel welcome!" He put his hands together, encouraging the audience to do the same. Raven heard a desultory sprinkling of applause.

Her legs refused to move. She squeezed her eyes shut. Her throat constricted around the hard wad of dread she tried to force down.

Hunter's words came to her. *You don't know those people out there.*

Raven opened her eyes, saw Hunter giving her an encouraging wink from the stage. He was right. Who cared what those people thought of her? She had to do this, if only to prove to herself that she could, to establish some measure of control over this stupid, debilitating fear.

Forcing herself to put one wobbly leg in front of the other, she made the long trek across the wooden stage. The spotlights blinded her; the audience was a blur. Hunter pressed the microphone into her trembling hands, gave her shoulder a friendly pat and was gone.

As Raven faced the faceless audience, gut-wrenching panic wiped her mind clean. Desperately she cast around for a coherent thought, and found herself latching on to Hunter's words.

Pretend you're talking to Amanda and Charli and Sunny. Just to them.

Mentally she focused on their table, knowing generally where it was, although she couldn't see it. She imagined chatting with her closest friends, sharing observations about life, love and men.

She heard herself say, "That last act reminded me of my first blind date."

Where the heck had that come from? That wasn't what she was supposed to say! She'd practiced her opening line over and over until it was hardwired into her brain—a comment about turning thirty unmarried—but for some reason, when she'd opened her mouth, something entirely different had popped out.

A ripple of laughter greeted her words—more a testament to how much they'd despised the last act than how much they liked her, Raven knew. Meanwhile she grappled for an entré into her rehearsed routine.

But the thing was, she *had* gone out with a man just like that. And so, she suspected, had many of the women in the audience. Which prompted her to add, "Guys like that are an acquired taste. Like getting your legs waxed."

This was rewarded with a burst of laughter, with higher-pitched female voices predominating. Raven's death grip on the mike slackened. She willed herself to relax fractionally.

"This blind date's name was Jerome," Raven said. "Jerome was so dense..." She paused meaningfully. When the audience failed to respond to this prompt the way Charli, Sunny and Amanda always did, she repeated, with exaggerated patience and broad gestures, *"Jerome was so dense..."*

They caught on. "How dense was he?" they hollered, more or less in unison.

"Jerome was so dense, he thought carpe diem meant 'fish of the day.'"

This was met with both chuckles and groans, but they were the kind of good-natured groans that told her her gag had hit the mark. Even the less literate in the audience had to know the Latin expression had nothing to do with seafood.

In that instant Raven realized Hunter was right. It wasn't so much what she said as the way she said it. The pacing, the pauses, the inflection—it all came naturally to her.

A detail from another blind date flashed through her mind. "The first thing out of Jerome's mouth was, 'I hope you have exact change for the bus.'"

She continued to rummage her memory stores, grafting bits and pieces from her long history of horrid dates onto her monologue about Jerome. This material segued seamlessly into her original "thirty and alone" topic.

She discussed how, once she turned thirty, she became the official spinster aunt of the family. "I'm learning the ropes," she said proudly. "The other day I offered my nephew a piece of linty ribbon candy from the bottom of my purse."

Her hands still shook, her palms sweated, her heart thumped like a bass drum, but she was doing it! She was opening her mouth and words were coming out—real words that made sense and, most remarkably, made the audience laugh and sometimes even clap.

Raven was surprised when the green traffic light at

the rear of the room turned yellow—her one-minute warning. She'd been talking for four minutes already!

She wrapped up her routine quickly, and the audience broke into spirited applause. Hunter materialized by her side. He asked the crowd, "Do we want Raven to return?" The enthusiastic response left no doubt that they did.

Raven blew a kiss to the audience and strode into the offstage waiting area, where, eyes closed, she collapsed against the nearest wall, gulping air, dizzy with relief.

I did it! I did it!

Vaguely she heard Hunter naming the headliners scheduled to perform that weekend, and bidding the patrons good-night.

I did it! I did it! I—

Her eyes snapped open when a firm, swift kiss landed on her mouth.

Hunter's eyes sparked with exhilaration and pride. "You did it!" he crowed, and kissed her again, clearly caught up in the excitement of the moment. Their giddy laughter mingled, then melted as their lips shifted, and parted, and clung.

Raven was only dimly aware of Hunter crushing her to the wall, of her hands sliding up his hard shoulders to pull him closer. Her senses were jumbled, her mind overloaded, reeling from the emotional roller coaster she'd ridden that evening. At that moment she didn't think, couldn't think, could only feel, and what she felt right then was the sweet, unadulterated rightness of it.

Hunter pressed closer until she was sandwiched, almost painfully, between the cold wall and his sinewy heat. He cupped the back of her neck and kissed her hard and deep, as if loath to release her, loath to relinquish the wonder of the moment and face the consequences.

Those consequences swooped in for the kill the instant they parted, breathless. Raven touched her lips, tender and swollen under her trembling fingertips. The taste of him lingered, stirring her senses. She girded her courage and made herself look Hunter in the eye. And wished she hadn't. His stricken expression cut like a knife blade.

He backed up a step, shook his head as if to disavow what had just happened. "Raven, I'm—"

"Don't." She couldn't bear to hear him apologize for that mind-blowing kiss.

He turned away, raking his fingers through his hair. "I didn't plan that. I would never—" Cursing, he kicked the janitor's bucket into a stack of cartons. He leaned a palm on the opposite wall, head bowed. In a voice tight with strain, he said, "I would never betray my brother."

"I know that." Raven's voice shook. She hugged herself. "I wouldn't either. What happened just now—it was no one's fault. It was the excitement, the relief, it just kind of...took over." She dragged in a shuddering breath and told the lie that Hunter needed to hear. "It didn't mean anything."

Slowly he straightened. He turned and looked her in

the eye, as if to gauge her sincerity. After a few seconds she had to look away.

His quiet words had a note of finality. "We'll forget this happened." When she didn't respond, he added, "Can you do that?"

Raven nodded. She cleared her throat. "Yes. Of course."

After a few moments Hunter took a tentative step toward her. "Raven..."

She looked up then, wearing a forced smile that cost her more than he could ever know. "Listen, don't worry about it," she said lightly. "It's not like we tore each other's clothes off. Things got a little out of hand, we both feel lousy about it and it'll never happen again. End of story."

7

HUNTER SIPPED single-malt Scotch and watched Kirsten undress. Comfortably ensconced in one of a pair of overstuffed armchairs her parents had parted with when she'd gotten her own apartment, he was digesting the roast pork and mashed potatoes she'd made for him. The glass he drank from was a burger-joint giveaway emblazoned with animated characters from the latest Disney movie.

"I'm thinking of going for my M.B.A.," Kirsten said, as she pulled the scrunchie out of her hair and shook out the chestnut waves.

"What would you do with an M.B.A.?" Hunter asked as she lifted the hem of her multicolored wool sweater and pulled it over her head, revealing a lithe torso clad only in a snug, tank-style undershirt. Her lovely high, small breasts pushed against the ribbed pink fabric. Hunter knew from experience just how firm and responsive those breasts were.

"Without an advanced degree, I'm pretty much at a dead end careerwise," she said, as she opened the fly of her jeans. Kirsten was administrative assistant to the director of sales of a large sporting goods company. "Everyone's getting promoted around me."

Hunter watched her step out of her jeans, watched as those firm, athletic legs came into view. Her pink bikini underpants matched her tank top, but clashed with the droopy orange socks that adorned her feet.

"You're cold," he announced. "Ask me how I can tell."

Kirsten glanced down at her chest. "How do you know I'm not, like, all sexed up and ready for you?"

"At the moment, you're more interested in M.B.A.s than the contents of my B.V.D.s." He tossed back the last of his Scotch and set the glass on the side table, on top of an issue of *Shape Magazine.* "Come here."

She took a running leap and propelled herself onto his lap, squirming in place to straddle him. There were times when Hunter felt ancient and worn-out in the face of Kirsten's seemingly inexhaustible energy. He chafed the gooseflesh from her arms as she lowered her head and kissed him.

"It's been a while," she murmured. "You work too many hours. I'm surprised you let Matt cover for you tonight."

"You can't grow a business by treating it like a nine-to-five job."

"That's why I'll never own my own business." She started working on the buttons of his indigo denim shirt. "I'd rather work for someone else and know I have a paycheck coming every two weeks. What's this? No undershirt. Mmm..." She trailed her fingers through the chest hair exposed by his open shirt, then bent down to nip at his shoulder—one of his most reliable "on" buttons.

He should have been completely relaxed by now, after that heavy dinner and the double shot of whiskey. Unfortunately, the only part of him that was relaxed was the one part that shouldn't be, with a sexy twenty-one-year-old nymphet crawling all over him.

Okay, *nymphet* wasn't fair; he knew that. Kirsten wasn't underage, after all, no matter how much she might look it. Hunter recalled Raven's comment about Kirsten borrowing ID to go wine-tasting.

She raised her head. "What are you snickering about?"

"I wasn't snickering. Don't stop." He pulled her closer. "I like what you were doing."

"Really? You seemed…somewhere else."

"I'm a little tense, is all. Work." It was a lie, but what was he supposed to tell her? *I nearly jumped my brother's woman and it's got me just a tad on edge.*

It's not like we tore each other's clothes off, Raven had said. He couldn't speak for her, but for him it was a close thing. As far as she was concerned, the excitement of the moment had taken over and things had just gotten a little out of hand. *It didn't mean anything.* Her words.

If that was how she really felt—and he wasn't entirely convinced it was—then he was glad for her sake. She hadn't done anything wrong, after all. He was the one who'd initiated that kiss. He was the one who'd gone overboard and turned what should have been a congratulatory peck into a damn tonsil-hockey tournament.

The thought of tournaments triggered another, troubling memory. What was that business about Brent missing his girlfriend's first, scary foray into stand-up comedy to play cards? Hunter wasn't privy to every detail of his brother's social life, but that had been the first he'd heard of a poker tournament. Raven had needed support, encouragement, a hand to hold. If she were Hunter's, nothing would have kept him from her side at a time like that.

He'd encouraged her to continue performing at Stitches, and to her credit, she'd agreed. Yesterday she'd stepped onstage for the second time, with different material. She'd still been anxious, of course, and there had been a few shaky moments during her routine, but she'd done a creditable job—on her own this time, with no little ploys from him to help her along. For her first performance, he'd put her on after the audience had been loosened up, and had made sure she'd followed a couple of losers, so she couldn't help but look terrific by comparison.

"Well, don't worry," Kirsten said, as she lightly tugged on his chest hair. "By the time I'm finished with you, you won't be tense at all. I guarantee it."

He gave her the suggestive smile he knew she expected. "So I should put myself in your hands, is that it?"

"For starters." She gyrated on his lap. If she expected

that to make him into an upstanding citizen, she was destined for disappointment.

Hunter had to take corrective action, and fast. He'd never had a problem getting hard, and he damn sure didn't intend to start now!

He closed his eyes and took a deep breath as Kirsten's hands slid up his chest, out to his shoulders and down again in a soothing circular pattern. Automatically he started the process of relaxation Raven had taught him, imagining himself on the beach, feeling the tension ebb from each part of his body in turn.

His first impulse after last week's illicit kiss had been to cancel his second hypnotherapy session scheduled for the following morning. But his good intentions—not to mention his good sense—had succumbed to his over-whelming desire to spend that stolen hour with Raven, and in the end, he'd kept his appointment.

As he felt his muscles loosen and his breathing slow, Hunter recalled Raven's voice as it had sounded that very morning during his third session, throaty and coaxing. He remembered how exotic she'd looked, in a loose, calf-length dress printed with a Moroccan-looking pattern in warm earth tones. The fluid fabric had drifted around her body in a most distracting way. Even when she'd sat primly in the rocker in her office, with the notebook balanced on her crossed leg, he'd had to force himself to close his eyes and begin the pro-cess of deep relaxation. He could have looked at her all day.

And even then, it was Raven he'd seen behind his

closed eyelids, stretching out on the beach towel next to him, wearing a tiny bikini and asking him to undo her top so she wouldn't have tan lines.

The instant Hunter had begun to feel himself stir down there, he'd mentally booted Raven off his private beach. That was all he needed, after what had happened last week at Stitches—to get a conspicuous erection during his therapy session.

Now, however, he allowed himself to indulge in the fantasy he'd squelched that morning. He was back at the beach with Raven. It was her bare thighs warming his lap as she straddled him, her hands spreading suntan oil on his chest, up, out, down, over and over. She'd left her bikini top off, and her bare breasts, glistening with oil, swayed temptingly near his face. Her hips rocked into his as she massaged him.

Raven's smile was bewitching. "I need you, Hunter," she whispered. "I need you now. Make love to me." She ground herself against him, against the painfully stiff erection trying to hammer its way out of his swim trunks. He slid his hands up her bare thighs, groaning with the glut of carnal sensation. She was here and she wanted him, and all he had to do was push aside some scraps of cloth...

"Rest assured," she purred, "I've got nothing on my mind now but the contents of your B.V.D.s."

She kissed Hunter, startling him out of his hypnotic reverie. He was left gasping and disoriented, with a runaway heartbeat and a blue-ribbon hard-on.

It was Kirsten's lips pressed to his, Kirsten's thighs under his groping fingers.

"Whoa," she said. "Were you drifting off?"

She shimmied off his lap and settled on the carpet between his legs. When she reached for the distended fly of his jeans, Hunter bolted upright and grabbed her hands.

She looked up at him. "What's wrong?"

Stopping her had been an automatic response. He thought about it now, thought about making love to Kirsten. God knew that, physically, he needed the release. He should let her undress him, let her take him into her body, let her fill in for the woman who'd aroused him when she couldn't.

Not that Kirsten had ever failed to turn him on before. It wasn't her fault he was hung up on a woman he couldn't have. He knew for a fact that if he had sex with Kirsten now, he'd be thinking about Raven. Not the worst sin, perhaps, but it went against his grain. Which was why he'd stopped her.

He had to go with his gut. "I'm sorry, Kirsten. I think I'd better leave."

She stared at him wide-eyed for a moment, then stood and snatched her jeans off the carpet.

Hunter rose. "It's not you. God, that sounds so insipid," he groaned, "but it's true."

Kirsten wasn't stupid. "All you had to do was tell me you'd found someone, Hunter." She pulled her pants up and zipped them.

"That's not it—exactly."

She responded with a look that said, *Yeah, right.* The two of them didn't have an exclusive relationship—they were both free to see other people, and did.

She said, "So if there's no one special person you're saving it for, why the sudden freeze-out?" She paused in the act of putting on her sweater. "You don't have anything...?"

"No! It's nothing like that." Hunter got regular blood tests, always negative, and always used condoms to make sure it stayed that way. He sighed. "Okay. There's someone. But it's...messy."

"She married?"

"Something like that. I didn't think it would affect what you and I have."

Kirsten retrieved Hunter's black down jacket from her coat closet and held the apartment door open for him. "Let me know when you get over Mrs. Unavailable."

8

BRENT ANSWERED his doorbell on the third ring, wearing a thick white terry robe, a headful of rumpled hair and a huge yawn. "Hey, Bro. What time is it?"

"Almost ten-thirty. Did I get you out of bed?" Hunter deposited Brent's Sunday *New York Times*, which he'd retrieved from the porch, on the coffee table next to two empty wineglasses. He shed his parka and flopped on the sofa. "You're usually an early riser, even on Sundays. I thought you'd be up by now."

"Shh!" Brent padded to his bedroom door and silently closed it. He kept his voice low. "I've got company."

Something wrenched inside Hunter. He shouldn't have been surprised. Brent and Raven had been together for just over three weeks, and clearly it was getting serious. Hell, as far as Hunter knew, they might have been sleeping together since their first date.

He'd been prepared to treat Brent to the local brewpub brunch, but now all he wanted was to get out of there. The prospect of making small talk with a sleepy-eyed Raven over eggs Benedict after she'd spent the night with his brother was more than he could stomach at the moment. Seeing them cozy up to each other at

Brent's Super Bowl party last Sunday had been enough of a strain. They'd snuggled, teased each other, and in all respects appeared to be an established couple.

"Listen," Hunter said, rising. "I don't want to intrude. If I'd known you weren't alone—"

"You're not intruding." Brent lowered his voice even further. "The truth is, I'm kind of glad you showed up. Makes it easier to show her the door."

"What?"

"You know how it is," Brent said, idly flipping through the various sections of the Sunday *Times*. "Sometimes they can't take a hint. The morning after, it's like they're settled in for the duration. I've got things to do today. Hey, check it out." He picked up the travel section. "The cruise issue."

"You're trying to *get rid of her?*"

"Shh! Keep your voice down."

A drowsy female voice interrupted. "Brent?"

An olive-skinned beauty stood in the open doorway of Brent's bedroom, wearing only a man's white undershirt, which barely reached the tops of her long, long legs. She had exotic almond-shaped eyes and glossy black hair that fell to her hips. She smiled at Hunter. "Hi. I'm Marina."

Speechless, Hunter let his brother introduce him.

"I'm gonna hop in the shower," Marina said. "Will you be here when I get out?" she asked Hunter.

"Uh...I don't think so."

"Well, it was nice to meet you." She waggled her fingers at him and closed the bedroom door.

Hunter stared at his brother.

Brent grinned salaciously. "She's a *swimsuit model.* Met her at the health club."

"What the hell are you doing, Brent?"

"What do you mean?" Brent headed into the kitchen. Hunter followed him. "What about Raven?"

"What about her?"

"I thought you were serious about her."

"I am serious about her." Brent filled the coffeemaker with water. "I took her flying yesterday afternoon. We had a lot of fun. This has nothing to do with Raven."

"Somehow I don't think she'd see it that way." Hunter heard the whisper of water through pipes as Marina turned on the shower in the master bathroom.

"Why are you so riled? I'm no choirboy and neither are you."

"Raven seems to think the two of you have a real relationship."

"We do. You think I feel the same way about that girl—" Brent jerked his head toward his bedroom "—as I do for Raven? Marina's just a fun time. I'll probably see her once or twice more, tops."

"And what about Raven? Is she seeing other guys?"

Brent's look of exaggerated patience scraped Hunter's nerves. "What do you think?"

Hunter said, "I think if you were as serious about her as you claim, you wouldn't be nailing other women." Raven had told Hunter that she'd never betray Brent, and he believed her.

Brent slammed the grounds basket into the coffeemaker. "Where do you get off preaching to me? You're one to talk."

"At least I never misled anyone. If I had something special going with one woman, I wouldn't run around on her."

Brent leaned against the counter and crossed his arms. "That's assuming you were getting it from that someone special."

"What do you mean?"

"I mean Raven's not ready to sleep with me. Okay? She wants to wait and I'm cool with that. Hell, I'm more than cool with it—how often do you run across a girl with old-fashioned values like that nowadays? I'm thinking she may be the one. The future Mrs. Brent Radley."

Hunter's visceral relief that Raven hadn't yet given herself to Brent warred with outrage over his brother's lack of moral fiber. Hunter had always looked up to Brent, eight years his senior, though his childhood idolization had long since matured into admiration and camaraderie. At the moment, though, Hunter saw little to admire.

At least he now had a good idea what Brent had been doing the last two Wednesday nights while Raven bravely confronted her phobia at Stitches. No doubt he'd seen those evenings as opportunities to mess around with other women.

Hunter knew Raven felt guilty for responding to his kiss. He almost wished she'd find out what Brent had been up to—except that it would hurt her. For that reason and his damnable family loyalty, Hunter would keep his mouth shut.

He said, "You two have only been together three weeks. You couldn't have waited, too?"

"There's no telling how long it'll be. Sex is a big deal to Raven. I respect her too much to pressure her."

"But you don't respect her enough to wait with her."

"I take it back," Brent snapped, pushing off the counter and stalking to the cabinet where he kept coffee mugs. "You *have* turned into some kind of damn choirboy. I'm not hurting Raven. If anything, it's good for our relationship, my getting it somewhere else. Like a pressure valve. Makes it easier for me to back off and give her the time she needs."

"Listen to yourself. Tell me that doesn't sound like the self-serving rationalization it is."

Brent responded with a raw oath.

Hunter advanced on him. "Is that what you'll tell yourself if you two get married? When the honeymoon's over and you find yourself slipping around on the side? That it's good for your marriage, that you're doing your wife some kind of fav—"

"Enough!" Brent slammed a coffee mug on the counter. "What is this to you? That's what I want to know. Why can't you just let it go?"

Brent glared at Hunter, who met his gaze unflinchingly—until something shifted behind Brent's eyes, ever so subtly, and then Hunter had to restrain the urge to back up. He tried to adopt a neutral expression, but he'd never been able to bluff where his brother was concerned.

A vein stood out on Brent's forehead. When he spoke at last, his voice was dangerously subdued. "You got something to tell me, little brother?"

Hunter held his gaze as long as he could before looking away.

Brent got right in Hunter's face. "Answer me, damn it. If you don't, I'll find out from Raven—"

"No. Don't bring her into this."

"You're my brother," Brent snarled between clenched teeth. "I trusted you."

"Look, it's nothing, Brent. I swear."

"*What's* nothing?"

Hunter sighed. "Okay. If I'd met her first... But I didn't. That's all. No big deal."

"Yeah, no big deal," Brent scoffed. "Never knew you had a thing for older women. Does she know how you feel?"

"No, and it's going to stay that way."

Brent's color was high; he controlled himself with a conspicuous effort. "You are not going to be alone with her anymore, you got that?" He stabbed a finger at Hunter's chest. "Tell her you don't want her doing any more stand-up at Stitches."

"What?"

"You heard me."

"Brent, listen, it's done wonders for her, getting up onstage, speaking in front—"

"It's done wonders for you, too, huh?" Brent sneered.

"What do you imagine could happen at the club?" Hunter assumed his most guileless expression, though he'd already found out what could happen at the club. "Even if I were going to make a move on Raven—which I'm not—the place is packed on Wednesday nights. I'm running a damn restaurant and coordinating dozens of acts, for God's sake!"

"Forget it." Brent sliced a hand through the air. "If I'm not there, she's not there."

Hunter wondered how Brent would react if he knew about the private hypnotherapy sessions, about the special plans he and Raven had for this coming Thursday. His chest felt too tight to draw in a full breath. He'd never gone head-to-head with Brent on something this heavy, and all he wanted now was to slither away and forget it had happened.

But it had, and in his gut he knew his relationship with his brother would never be the same.

Hunter tried reason. "Don't punish Raven because of me. She needs to get up onstage. It boosts her confidence and she loves it."

"This is not negotiable. She's through with it, as of now."

"Then you'll have to be the one to tell her. But don't be surprised if she tells you to go to hell. Raven doesn't seem like the kind of woman you can order around. Especially when the order doesn't make any damn sense."

"Tell her you have to give other people a turn," Brent persisted. Coldly he added, "You owe me."

Hunter stared at his brother, hoping he'd heard wrong, knowing he hadn't. Never would he have expected Brent to hold that over his head. Quietly he said, "This has nothing to do with what I owe you."

"Maybe I don't see it that way."

Hunter took a deep breath. "Look. This whole thing is so stupid. I told you, it's nothing. Tell me you've never thought about a buddy's woman that way. It doesn't mean you'd do anything about it."

Brent's scowl deepened. "Family's different."

"Okay, so you have my permission to think dirty thoughts about Lauren and Kirsten and Rachel and—"

"Shut the hell up," Brent muttered, his tone more weary now than outraged. He scrubbed a hand over his bristly jaw. "I don't know what to do about this."

"You don't have to do anything about it," Hunter said. "Don't blow it out of proportion. I'm not obsessed. I'm not in love. And next week I'll probably say, 'Raven Who?'"

The muffled sound of the shower ceased. Moments later Marina called through the closed bedroom door, "What are we doing about breakfast? Hey, I know this great natural-foods place that has outstanding wheat-grass juice and veggie burgers. And later this afternoon I thought we could go to that miniatures museum in Roslyn. Did I tell you I collect dollhouse furniture?"

Brent slumped against the fridge, looking as forlorn as Sisyphus watching that big rock roll back down the hill.

"Wheatgrass juice," Hunter said, as he headed out of the kitchen. "Is that what swimsuit models drink?"

"You're not cutting out on me now!" Brent snatched at Hunter's shirtsleeve. "Help me get rid of her. Tell her we have to visit Grandma in the nursing home or something."

"How about we all go visit Grandma at her condo instead. She can show Marina her collection of miniature liquor bottles and motel shampoos."

"This isn't like you, Hunter. You could help me out if you wanted to. I'd do it for you."

"What can I tell you? If you didn't want to deal with her the morning after, you should've gone to her place instead. 'Sleep well? Me, too. So long.'" *Or you could've kept it in your pants and we wouldn't be having this discussion,* Hunter thought as he let himself out the front door. He wanted to make things right with his brother, but not by making it easier for him to cheat on Raven.

He turned to say goodbye, only to have the door slam shut in his face.

9

"YOU KNOW, you're doing very well." Raven watched Hunter's profile as he calmly took in the spectacle before them. "Surprisingly well. You should be proud of yourself."

He smiled at her. "I owe it all to my therapist."

They stood on the indoor observation deck on the 107th floor of the World Trade Center, located at the southern tip of Manhattan. This, of course, was the tallest skyscraper in New York, not counting the slightly higher twin tower next door, and this visit was the culmination of a day of hands-on therapy for Hunter. At the end of last week's hypnotherapy session, Raven had informed him he was ready to test his progress in the field, by deliberately exposing himself to heights. He'd balked until she'd offered to clear her schedule and accompany him, at which point he'd immediately agreed to the outing.

They'd driven to Manhattan and spent the day scaling a variety of towering structures. They'd started out, tamely enough, riding the glass elevators in the Times Square Marriott Hotel, over and over. Hunter had made himself stare out the glass back as the elevator rose and the hotel's atrium receded far below. He'd held on to Raven tightly as she'd talked him through the ordeal, reinforcing his newfound sense of control and equilibrium, urging him to be in touch with his body and his center of gravity, giving him mental tricks to help him cope.

From there they'd moved on to the Empire State Building observation deck, the Statue of Liberty, and finally the World Trade Center. Hunter appeared to be gaining mastery over his acrophobia. He forced himself to linger at each lofty location, although he still needed to keep his arm firmly around his therapist.

Not that Raven objected. Perhaps she should have. After what had happened two weeks ago at Stitches, perhaps she should have adopted an attitude of detached professionalism and resisted any physical contact. But she couldn't bring herself to do that. It wasn't her style to be so aloof, but more than that, this was Hunter, and it just felt too damn good having his arm around her.

It wasn't as if it could lead to a repeat performance of that amazing kiss. They'd spent the day in very public places, cheek to jowl with scores of tourists, and anyway, they both knew that kiss had been a fluke and would never happen again.

Except in that netherworld between wakefulness and sleep, when she lay in her solitary bed and her groggy mind drifted into forbidden territory. Then she felt him again, and tasted him again, and it was right again, so right. And there was no Brent and no Wedding Ring pact and it was only her and Hunter....

Raven had to keep reminding herself that not only was Hunter her client—and strictly off-limits for that reason alone—but he was the brother of the man she was committed to dating for a full three months, as long as Brent remained interested.

And he seemed to be getting more interested by the day—whereas her own feelings were harder to pin down. Brent was intelligent, fun-loving and thoughtful. He respected her desire to take things slow, accepted the fact that she wasn't ready for a physical relationship.

Raven suspected that if Hunter weren't in the picture, she'd be head over heels in love with his brother by now. But as it was, the situation was too confusing. She needed time to sort it out. Under the circumstances, the three-month rule was probably a good thing.

"Brent told me he took you flying on Saturday," Hunter said.

"It was incredible!" Raven nodded toward a small white airplane visible in the sky some distance below them. "That was us. We took off from a commercial airport in Jersey and flew up the west side of Manhattan. It was a little rocky and I started turning green around the gills, but the experience was unbelievable."

Hunter chuckled. "I always cross myself when we take off and land—and I'm not even Catholic!"

Raven's eyes widened. "You've gone flying with him? What about your acrophobia?"

"I...didn't want Brent to know about my fear of

heights. So I kind of toughed it out. Kept my eyes shut a lot."

"And crossed yourself a lot." She smiled. "Whatever works."

She couldn't imagine how Hunter had managed those jaunts in a small airplane, which she knew from experience entailed sitting in a tiny cabin right in front of the windshield, looking down, down, down.... There was a whole lot of down when you were in one of those things.

The observation deck they stood on ran nearly the entire perimeter of the 107th floor, while the interior housed gift shops and a food court. Viewers could stand at the railing, or step down through cutouts in the railing to sit on benches closer to the Plexiglas walls that provided a panoramic view.

Visibility was remarkable on this afternoon in early February. Facing south, they clearly saw Battery Park straight down; the Statue of Liberty, Ellis Island, Governors Island and Staten Island; and the Atlantic Ocean stretching into the distance. To their left was the East River and Brooklyn, to their right, the Hudson River and New Jersey.

Raven looked at Hunter, who was clearly absorbed by the bird's-eye view. A frown puckered her brow. He experienced occasional moments approaching panic, interspersed with periods of utter calm. It was almost as if he could turn his acrophobia on and off at will. Either that or he'd become proficient at disguising his symptoms.

Any other explanation didn't bear close scrutiny.

With the slightest touch, Hunter urged her to continue their stroll around the observation deck. They passed people of all races and nationalities, conversing in a dozen tongues. A man speaking an Eastern Europe language Raven couldn't identify dropped a coin in the binoculars mounted for public use and lifted his small son so he could look into them.

Hunter steered her around a knot of teenagers speaking French. "You know, you did real well last night. You appeared entirely comfortable onstage."

"I did? I was a wreck. I'm always a wreck, but it's getting better. My legs don't shake so much."

"At least Brent finally got to catch your act. What kept him away last week? He said he was sick, right?"

Raven nodded. "I offered to cancel my gig at Stitches to come over and take care of him, but he wouldn't let me. He said all he needed was rest, that he was going to go straight to bed and stay there."

Hunter made a funny noise deep in his throat.

"Oh, don't worry, he's fine now," Raven assured him. "Turned out to be just one of those twenty-four-hour bugs, thank goodness. The weird thing is, on Sunday he called and asked me out for last night. Which I thought was a little odd, considering we really haven't gone out on weeknights and he knows how I spend every Wednesday night nowadays."

"Doing stand-up therapy."

She laughed. "Dr. Radley's amazing cure. Anyway, Brent was kind of insistent about my taking the night

off to be with him, which really isn't like him." She
shrugged. "At least I don't think it is. I mean, I was willing to miss a performance to take care of him when he
was sick. But just for a dinner date we could have anytime?"

"Let me guess. You stuck to your guns and in the end
he decided to join you at Stitches."

"That's right, and he had this lovely surprise for me
after the show! Two dozen yellow roses. Can you believe it? You must've helped him hide them."

"Stashed 'em in my office."

"I guessed as much. Anyway, I thought it was really
sweet of him." It would have been sweeter, though, to
have had Brent's presence at her first two perform-
ances, flowers or no flowers. Raven instantly admonished herself. He'd wanted to be there last week; it
wasn't his fault he'd gotten sick.

As they strolled toward the north-facing part of the
observation deck, the entire island of Manhattan lay
spread out before them. Raven recognized the Empire
State Building and the slanted pinnacle of the Citicorp
Center. Sunlight glinted off the art deco spire of the
Chrysler Building and the gold dome of the Metropoli-
tan Life Building.

Hunter slid his arm around Raven, prompting her to
ask, "How are you managing?"

"I'm okay. It helps, having you with me."

"I guess it's like the way I felt the first time I per-
formed at the club. You got me to do something I never
in a million years would have thought I could do. You

never let me chicken out. You were always there, encouraging me, coaching me, giving me a verbal kick in the pants when I needed it." She grinned. "My own private drill sergeant."

As they watched, clouds drifted over Manhattan, casting living shadows on the landscape of buildings.

"Look at that," Raven breathed. "It's...surreal."

"'All that we see or seem,'" Hunter recited, staring at the remarkable vista, "'Is but a dream within a dream.'"

She smiled. "More Poe."

He was quiet for a long moment. Without looking at her, he said, "I wonder if you know how much you reveal about yourself when you go out on that stage."

"I guess I never really thought about it. Should I be worried?" she joked.

Hunter turned and leaned back against the railing, so he was facing Raven instead of the window. He folded his arms over his chest. "I have a feeling I gain as much insight into you, just from listening to your routines, as you do about me during my hypnotherapy sessions."

She thought about her acts, the wry observations about family, friends and romantic relationships. She couldn't help asking, "So tell me. What have you learned about Raven Muldoon?"

Hunter was mere inches away. His black down jacket lay open over a white turtleneck. His big body radiated heat and a subtle and alluring masculine scent. Raven fought an almost irresistible urge to slide her hands under his jacket, to lean into him, to cling to him and feel his arms band tightly around her....

"What have I learned about Raven?" Hunter mused, as though to himself. "I've learned that Raven is an inherent optimist, a Pollyanna in a world of cynicism and self-indulgence."

"A Pollyanna! Oh God!" She dropped her head into her hands.

Grinning, he pulled her hands away from her face and held them. "I've learned that Raven has a solid moral core, and if the rest of humanity is determined to go to hell, she sees no reason to follow them there. I've learned that Raven is a generous and devoted friend. Just ask the pals she's had since kindergarten. I've learned that Raven is too bright and competent for most of the men she's been involved with."

"You can stop now."

"She puts on a good front," he continued, "but lately she's begun to wonder if *she's* the reason she's thirty and single." He cocked his head, studying her intently. "I've learned that Raven has all this love bottled up inside, just waiting for the right recipient."

Raven's eyes stung. Mortified, she ducked her head. Hunter tugged her closer still. The rough pads of his thumbs swiped away the tears before they could fall. He cradled her face and tilted it up. "My brother doesn't know what a treasure he has."

This close, Hunter's warm breath teased her lips, and she could almost taste him again. As if she'd spoken the thought aloud, his gaze dropped to her mouth, and for one mad, reckless second she thought, *Yes, do it, don't think about it, just do it.*

A muscle twitched in his jaw and he dragged his bleak gaze back to her eyes. He released her. She backed up a step, drew a shaky breath. At once her surroundings snapped into sharp focus: the throngs, the noise. The smell of pizza and french fries from the food court. The sprawling cityscape far below.

Raven looked away for a few seconds. When she felt in control of her voice, she said, "Still want to tackle the rooftop walkway? It's pretty nippy out there. Seven below with the windchill factor."

"I'm up for it if you are."

"Great. Let's do it." The bracing cold was probably just what she needed right now. From the way Hunter had looked at her a few moments ago, she suspected it was just what he needed, too.

Not for the first time, she thought, *Why can't anything be simple?* She started walking.

He tugged her arm to stop her. "Raven." His eyes reflected a heady brew of conflicting emotion. "You could stand to be a little more cynical and a little less trusting."

She let her frown ask what he meant by that.

Hunter directed his gaze over her shoulder. He jammed his hands in his jacket pockets, and Raven sensed a battle being waged within him. When he looked at her again, his expression was unreadable. "Forget it. I'm one to give advice, right? Let's check out the roof."

10

"IS THAT A NEW PIN?" Hunter eyed Raven's medieval-looking, heart-shaped brooch as he hung his jacket on the antique coat rack in the corner of her office.

"Brent gave it to me for Valentine's Day."

I should've known, Hunter thought.

She caressed the smooth, oval chunk of amber set in the brooch, which contrasted dramatically with her black sweater tunic. "I love amber. He gave me matching earrings, too." She tucked her hair behind her ears to show them off.

"Nice." Hunter reached out and lifted one dangling, amber-studded earring. His fingertips grazed Raven's earlobe. He sensed more than heard her breath catch.

He released the earring. Valentine's Day. He couldn't help but wonder if the romantic holiday had prompted Raven to consummate her relationship with his brother. Considering the fact that Brent had spent the next evening with Marina, Hunter doubted it.

This was his sixth hypnotherapy session. Two weeks earlier, on the blustery rooftop walkway of the World Trade Center, Raven had declared him, if not cured, then well on his way. He didn't need her anymore, she'd stated, her gaze fixed on the coastline of New Jersey. There was no need to schedule further sessions.

She'd been rattled at the time; he knew that. She must have sensed how close he'd come to kissing her again, downstairs on the observation deck. He knew he made her nervous as hell. But he hadn't been ready to give up his sessions with her. He'd come to depend on them, his Raven "fix," the high point of his week.

So he'd spouted those lies about how he put on a brave front, and it might not be obvious, but he still needed to work on his acrophobia. And she hadn't challenged him, even if, as he suspected, she was beginning to see through the charade.

It could be that she was bighearted enough to give him the benefit of the doubt.

Or it could be that she, too, looked forward to that one hour a week.

Like an addiction, she monopolized his thoughts during the long days when he didn't get to see her. And like an addiction, his dependence increased steadily, despite the fact that it could lead to nothing but heartache, despite what it was doing to his relationship with his brother, which he'd once considered sacrosanct.

Have a falling out with Brent over a woman? Before the last few weeks—before Raven—the very idea would have been laughable.

His interactions with Brent had been strained, to say the least, during the two and a half weeks since his brother had slammed the door in his face. And Brent still didn't know about these clandestine therapy sessions, augmenting the burden of guilt that weighed more heavily on Hunter with each passing day.

"You seem distracted," Raven said. "Is something wrong?"

"No." Hunter sat in the recliner. He tilted it back. "Let's just get started." Maybe then he could convince himself he had a legitimate reason for being here.

Raven collected her notebook, which Hunter thought of as her security blanket—a prop to help convince her, too, that theirs was an ordinary therapist-client relationship.

"Have you had any encounters with heights since our last session?" she asked, taking her usual place on her rocker.

"No."

"No tall office buildings, no—"

"No. Nothing." He shifted in the chair, trying to get comfortable.

"Okay, well...close your eyes, Hunter."

He did.

"You're at the beach," she said, "lying on your towel. You're listening to the rhythmic sound of the waves as they break on the shore. The warmth of the sun—"

"I can't do this." He opened his eyes.

"What is it? Are you too tense?" Raven set aside her notebook. She leaned toward him with tender concern. Her fresh, powdery scent wafted over him. "Would you like to talk for a few minutes?"

Hunter just looked at her. Finally he tilted the chair up. "I can't do this anymore."

She straightened. She said nothing, but watched him with wary eyes as he sat forward, elbows on knees, and shoved all ten fingers through his hair.

Quietly he said, "You know what I mean."

She held his gaze for a moment before looking at her lap.

"Don't tell me you don't," he said.

"Hunter..." She shook her head, as if to deny that things had gotten this far. When she spoke again, he had to strain to hear her. "I really hate this."

He sighed. A minute passed in total silence. Finally he said, "Did you ever wonder where I got the capital to open Stitches?"

"I guess I've wondered," she said. "It wasn't my business to ask." When he gave her a look that said, *Figure it out,* she said, "Brent?"

He nodded. "He cashed in some CDs, wiped out a couple of retirement accounts. Took a hell of a hit on early withdrawal penalties. He's not charging me a penny in interest, either. If it weren't for him, I'd be managing somebody else's business right now, and hoping I could save enough bread by the time I'm forty to buy in to it."

After a moment she said, "You feel beholden to your brother."

Hunter smiled wistfully. "That's the least of what I'm beholden to Brent for. He was eight years old when I was born. He practically raised me. By the time I came along—a happy accident, so I gather—my parents were middle-aged and preoccupied with their careers. Not that they neglected me or anything, but our sister, Tina, was already in school and, well, I guess the baby of the family always has to kind of work to find his place.

"Brent relished the job of big brother from day one. As far as he was concerned, I was his project, his responsibility. I used to toddle around after him, and all I wanted—" Hunter's throat was tight with emotion; his childhood adoration was still so vivid. "All I wanted was to be like him. To *be* him. He was everything I aspired to be." He looked at Raven. "Can you understand that?"

Raven nodded, her eyes glistening.

"When I was old enough to get into trouble, he always bailed me out," Hunter continued. The memory triggered a crooked grin. "I'd pick fights with everyone, knowing my big brother would step in and keep me from getting hurt. Until the day he decided I needed to learn a lesson. I was nine and I goaded the neighborhood thug-in-training until it came to blows. Brent stood on the sidelines, giving me one or two words of encouragement but otherwise staying out of it." Hunter laughed. "My nose didn't stop bleeding for hours. I never picked a fight again."

"That must've been hard for him," Raven said. "To stand there and watch his little brother take a pounding and not do anything to stop it."

"Years later Tina told me how shaken he'd been. But it was something he had to do. He watched to make sure I didn't get killed, but otherwise, I was on my own." He chuckled. "Son of a bitch."

Raven's smile was gentle. "He helped make you the man you are."

Hunter dragged in a deep, ragged breath. "I owe him a lot. And not just the money for the club, which I'll manage to repay someday. It's just...so much more."

"Hunter." Raven leaned forward. She placed her hand on his. "You haven't done anything wrong."

His response was a mirthless half laugh.

"You haven't," she insisted.

"He knows."

Raven started to pull her hand away. Hunter seized it, twined his fingers with hers.

"He knows how I feel about you," he said. "It came up because...well, it's not important. As far as he's concerned, you know nothing about it, and that's the way we're going to leave it." He searched her eyes. "Raven. I'm not trying to come between you and Brent. That was never my intention. I need you to know that."

"I never thought you were."

Slowly he released her fingers. "I won't be coming back here." He gave her a wry look. "Let's just say I've experienced a sudden and miraculous cure."

"I'll stop doing stand-up at Stitches."

"No! That's not... Listen, out of the two of us, you were the one with the actual phobia, and you've worked on it and you've come a long way toward conquering it. Damn it, you're not stopping now."

"This is why Brent has been trying to keep me from the club, isn't it? Because of you and me."

Hunter nodded.

"Does he know about the...I mean, that we..."

"The kiss? No. He just doesn't want us together when he's not around." Hunter sighed miserably. "He doesn't trust me."

"Or me."

"That's not true. Raven, he knows this is a one-sided thing." She started to speak and he cut her off. "It'd be just like you to try to deflect his ire from me by taking some of the blame yourself. All that would accomplish is to tear you two apart. This thing between me and Brent—I have to work on it myself."

"Hunter, it's more complicated than that."

"I know how you feel about Brent. I've watched the two of you together. Whatever you think you feel for me, it's not the same. It's a chemical thing—a superficial attraction. It'll pass."

Raven's voice wavered. "I'm not so sure about that."

"It'll pass," he insisted, "but meanwhile, if I weren't in the picture, you'd be sleeping with Brent by now—maybe even picking out a china pattern." Thinking of his brother's hypocrisy, he added, "Don't beat yourself up over this. Whatever you imagine your sins to be, they're nothing in the greater scheme of things. Not everyone holds himself to such high standards."

"I'm not the saint you seem to think I am."

Hunter stared at Raven sitting there, heartbreakingly lovely in the warm lamplight. No, not a saint, he thought. An angel. A golden angel. Stark sincerity shone in her eyes. She really believed she was flawed, perhaps even unworthy of Brent. For responding to

Hunter? He couldn't bear being the cause of her self-reproach.

"My brother doesn't deserve you," he murmured.

"You said something like that before. I wish you wouldn't."

"It's true."

"Why?"

Hunter tried to make the words come. But he couldn't. Brent was still his brother. Brothers didn't inform on each other. He shook his head helplessly.

Raven said evenly, "I know about the other women." She smiled gently at his stunned expression. "I'm not stupid, Hunter. And I'm no naive, besotted young thing. I've learned how to read the signs. It took a while to sink in because I guess I really didn't want to believe it."

"But if you know—" he spread his hands, struggling to fathom the unfathomable "—why are you still with him?"

Raven opened her mouth to reply, but the words died on a frustrated sigh. "I can't explain it."

"Maybe I can. You're blindly in love with a man who takes you for granted."

"No."

Hunter rose to his feet. "You tell me you're not naive, Raven, not besotted. But how else can you explain putting up with his cheating?"

"I'm not—not really. It's complicated. There are issues I have to...clarify. I need to talk to Amanda and the others. I really can't discuss it with you right now."

"Because I wouldn't understand, is that is? I can't possibly comprehend the depths of your devotion—"

"Hunter, stop it!"

He seized the back of her rocking chair with both hands, leaned over her until they were practically nose-to-nose. She shrank back.

"The man is cheating on you, Raven!"

"He...never promised fidelity."

Hunter made her look him in the eye. "Are you telling me the subject never came up?"

She hesitated.

"Let me guess," he said. "You told him he was the only one. Only, he didn't give you the same kind of assurance, did he? Maybe you inferred it at the time. Now you know better and you're hoping he'll change—"

Raven tried to rise. Hunter clamped his hands on her shoulders and held her in place. "What do you think—that if you just keep your mouth shut and tolerate it, that if you *love* him enough, you'll turn him around?"

She glared up at him, her body rigid. "Let go of me."

"You know he's lying to you. He didn't have any twenty-four-hour bug. He had a twenty-four-hour hot date, but he was truthful about one thing. He went to bed and stayed there—"

She grabbed his wrists and tried to wrench out of his grasp, to no avail. Breathing hard, she said, "A minute ago you had me and your paragon of a brother picking out a china pattern. Now you tell me I'm throwing myself away on a lying cheat."

"You may not have noticed, but I'm a little conflicted

where you're concerned." With quiet condemnation, Hunter added, "If you stay with him now, knowing what you know, you're a doormat." And he abruptly released her.

She sprang out of her chair and slammed her palms into his chest, shoving him backward with surprising strength. "How dare you!" she cried, as tears of fury gathered in her eyes. She lunged at him again and he captured her wrists. "What gives you the right to pass judgment on me!" she demanded, struggling to free herself.

The tears streaked down her face. Hunter lashed his arms around her, binding her tightly against him. She fought him, sobbing. He pressed his lips to her wet, hot cheeks.

"That's just it, angel," he said in a hoarse whisper. "I've got no rights where you're concerned, and it makes me mad as hell." He tipped her face up and kissed her quivering lips. "I wish to God I'd met you first," he murmured against her mouth. "I'd give anything..."

This kiss was different from the first one a month ago. This time he was fully aware of what he was doing. He was aware and he did it anyway, because this kiss would have to hold him for the rest of his life.

Raven tried to wrench away. Hunter backed her into the recliner and lowered them both onto it, tilting it nearly flat.

"Hunter...!" she gasped, stiff with shock as he imprisoned her under him.

"If you belonged to me, I'd never look twice at another woman." He captured her mouth again, framing her face with his hands. Raven lay trembling beneath him, clearly grappling with her own opposing impulses. Hunter knew she responded to him on a purely physical level, and at the moment, he was greedy enough to take advantage of that primitive attraction.

He shifted a little so that they lay snugly dovetailed in the narrow space, her calf-length skirt snarled around their tangled legs. The brooch Brent had given her poked Hunter, reminding him that he'd run out of excuses. He couldn't tell himself later that he'd simply lost his head, that he hadn't intended to kiss her this deeply or this long, or to touch her like this, sliding his hand up her hip and over her tunic to her breast.

He inhaled Raven's soft gasp, which became a muted whimper as he stroked and molded the pliant softness of her breast. The wide, notched neckline of her tunic had shifted, revealing a gleaming shoulder and a white lace bra strap. Hunter touched his mouth to her satiny shoulder and kissed his way to the hollow of her throat.

She clutched handfuls of his red denim shirtsleeves, neither clinging nor pushing him away. He stared into her slumbrous eyes as he dragged the hem of her tunic to her shoulders. Her lips parted, her fingers tightened on his sleeves, but she made no move to stop him. He released the front clasp of her white lace bra and spread it open. Raven averted her face, struggling, no doubt, with her own conscience.

Her breasts were even more beautiful than in his fantasies. He touched a fingertip to one erect nipple. Raven flinched as if in pain. He fondled her very lightly, stroking, plucking. Strangled sounds escaped her and she arched against him, prompting him to press even closer to her. She had to feel how hard he was.

She was exquisitely sensitive, responding to the subtlest touch. Hunter lowered his head and flicked his tongue over one stiff peak. Raven cried out sharply, bucking off the recliner. He held her down and tasted her again, lingeringly, savoring her. She panted, clutching him.

Her legs scissored restlessly. He pulled her knee over his hip and seized her bottom, fitting himself into the cradle of her thighs, grinding into her as he suckled her. Raven's hoarse cries echoed her frenzied movements. Her head whipped from side to side. She groaned his name, sounding both anguished and transported. In the next breath, she gasped, "Stop!"

She was teetering on the edge of orgasm, and panicking, he knew, but it was too late to stop, even if he were willing to let her. "No..." she moaned, even as her breath snagged and her body bowed and her hips hitched hard and fast against him. Hunter pressed his hand between her legs, kneading her through her skirt until she collapsed, breathless, shuddering.

He gathered her in his arms, tucked her face into the crook of his neck. Her tunic was still bunched under her arms, her bare, warm breasts pressed to his chest. He felt the staccato rhythm of her heart as it gradually slowed. The heady, womanly fragrance of her arousal mingled with her powdery perfume, pushing his self-control to the extreme. His aching penis howled for release, confined as it was in his snug jeans.

Raven's lashes tickled Hunter's throat as her eyes drifted open. Automatically his arms tightened around her. He was prepared to hear her weep, or curse him—or, more likely, curse herself. Instead she lay passively in his embrace.

Her hand rested on his chest. He lifted it and brushed his lips over her knuckles. He wished he knew what she was thinking, but he wouldn't ask. If she was consumed by shame, what solace could he offer her?

So he held her and fantasized that he had the right to do this—to love this woman and pleasure her and hold her and dream.

She stirred at last, and looked at him. Her eyes revealed nothing of the inner turmoil she had to be suffering. He stroked her disheveled hair off her face.

Calmly she said, "I won't be alone with you again."

"I know."

She watched him in silence for several moments and then rose on her elbow. Lightly she traced his face with her fingertips, as if committing it to memory. She kissed him, a solemn kiss imbued with all the frustrated longing of the past six weeks.

Her hand drifted below his waist, where his erection strained the worn denim of his jeans. He made a guttural sound as she lightly stroked him. "Raven..."

She pulled belt leather free of its buckle.

"What are you doing?" he asked tightly.

"I want to do for you what you did for me."

"You don't have to do that, angel." He laid his hand over hers, halting her.

"I told you, I want to."

More likely she felt obligated. Hunter couldn't escape the irony of it—she hadn't wanted to climax in his arms, had been clearly distressed when it had happened, and yet she felt compelled to reciprocate.

"I don't want you to," he said, threading his belt back into the buckle.

"Hunter—"

"I've given you enough to regret."

Hunter struggled to make sense of his own actions. Three weeks ago he'd turned down the favors of a nubile young lass because she wasn't the woman he loved. Now he refused to let the woman he loved gratify him, because she was doing it for the wrong reasons.

He never used to be so damn noble, and now that he'd gotten a taste of it, he didn't like it one bit.

Of course, there was noble and there was noble. He figured what he'd just done with his brother's woman kind of canceled out the rest of it.

He fastened Raven's bra, pulled down her tunic and got up from the recliner. She sat there watching as he slipped his jacket on. Perhaps the single-digit temperatures outside would cool his ardor. If not, there was always the option of a solo act once he got home—an option he'd exercised all too often these past weeks, thanks to his dormant love life.

As Hunter pulled on his gloves and prepared to

leave, the only thing he could think to say didn't bear saying.

Tell me I still didn't do anything wrong.

He leaned over Raven, kissed her on the forehead and let himself out of the house.

11

"JUST A SLIVER FOR ME," Amanda said.

Raven watched her friend's eyes pop as Grandma Rossi cut her a slab of Italian cheesecake that would choke a rhino.

"I said just a sliver!"

Grandma Rossi snorted as she plunked the heavily laden dessert plate in front of Amanda with a resounding thud.

Charli said, "Amanda, you've known my grandma for a quarter of a century. Have you ever known her to cut a sliver of anything?"

"You're too skinny." Grandma pinched Amanda's upper arm. "The men, they like something they can hold on to, *capisce?*"

She rested her plump, gnarled hand on Raven's shoulder. "How about you, little bird? You ready for seconds?"

"Little bird" had long been her pet name for Raven, although it was Grandma Rossi herself who bore a physical resemblance to a raven, widowhood having turned her wardrobe a uniform black nine years earlier. Otherwise she hadn't changed much over the years. Her iron-gray hair was still twisted into a tight bun on the back of her head, she still made the best gnocci in Queens and she still had an opinion on everything, most notably the disappointing marital status of her granddaughter and her friends.

Raven laid her hand on Grandma Rossi's. "Thanks, Mrs. Rossi, but I'm stuffed. Everything was delicious, as always."

Grandma Rossi squeezed her hand. "You're a good girl. How come you're not married?"

Raven grinned. "I can only tell you what I've told you the last couple of hundred times you've asked. I haven't found the right guy."

"My Carlotta, she tells me you got a fella. A nice boy. You get his ring on your finger, little bird. You're not getting any younger."

"I'm not so eager for this man's ring."

Grandma Rossi made a rude noise accompanied by a dismissive wave. She waddled to the dining room's ornate sideboard and lifted the carafe of espresso. Raven and her friends knew better than to insist the old lady sit and let them wait on themselves, and her. Grandma Rossi had moved in with Charli and her parents when Grandpa Rossi had passed away nine years earlier, and she fussed over the three of them with the same pugnacious zeal with which she'd fussed over her husband for six decades.

All this fussing did Grandma Rossi good, but in actual fact, the ninety-three-year-old needed plenty of fussing over herself, for everything from help getting dressed to remembering to take her potassium supplements.

And it wasn't just Grandma Rossi who needed assistance with day-to-day tasks. Her son and daughter-in-law, Charli's parents, were in their seventies, and it was a rare week when Charli wasn't called on to accompany one or both of them to the family doctor or some other specialist. She did the daily laundry and the weekly grocery shopping. She supervised medications, finances and the running of the house. All this on top of her career as a high school music teacher.

Charli was the youngest of eight siblings, her sisters and brothers all married and raising families of their own, ostensibly too busy to help care for the old folks. Thus the job of caretaker had naturally fallen to her, reinforced by her strict upbringing, which had taught her that the only acceptable move for a woman was from her parents' home to her husband's. "Nice" single women didn't set up their own households.

Raven knew that even if Charli didn't have to look after her folks, she considered herself too plain and timid to attract a husband. She also knew that it was with a mixture of trepidation and giddy anticipation that Charli looked forward to her thirtieth birthday in April, when she would become the object of the second Wedding Ring husband hunt.

"Well, *I* won't turn down seconds, Mrs. Rossi," Sunny said, handing over her plate. "Listen, Raven, if you don't want Brent, maybe I'll take a crack at him."

"I'm not so sure you'd want him, either."

Four sets of eyebrows lifted skyward. Raven knew what they were thinking. If her marriage-minded "stone hunk" possessed some fault that even Sunny would reject him for, it had to be bad news.

"So he's what?" Amanda asked. "A cannibalistic serial killer?"

"He's cheating on me."

Charli's jaw dropped. "That's terrible!"

Amanda uttered a disgusted huff and lifted her demitasse cup to her lips.

Grandma Rossi muttered something evil-sounding in Italian.

"Hmm," was all Sunny said.

"It's been going on for the whole two months we've been together," Raven continued. "Last weekend he went skiing at Catamount—an overnight outing with the guys, supposedly. Only, yesterday I was at his place, opening drawers looking for a coaster, and I came across these snapshots from the trip, and they're all of Brent cuddling up to this gorgeous woman with long black hair down to her skinny little butt.

"Anyway, under the circumstances, I think I should be released from the three-month rule."

Grandma Rossi knew about the three-month rule. She was the only outsider they'd let in on the Wedding Ring pact. She poured herself a cup of espresso, lowered her bulk into a dining chair and said, "Not so fast, little bird."

"What's the point in prolonging it?" Raven asked. "I'm not going to marry a man I can't trust."

"Maybe he'll change," Charli said.

Amanda sent Charli a look that said, *Get real.* "Take it from me. Cheating men don't change." Amanda hadn't been nearly so cynical before her two failed marriages.

"Let me ask you." Sunny propped her elbows on the table and leaned toward Raven. "Did you and Brent agree on an exclusive relationship?"

"Not exactly." Raven should have known Sunny would try to rationalize Brent's womanizing. Before her friend could get too smug, she added, "What I mean is, he made sure I wasn't seeing other guys, but he kind of evaded the issue himself."

"You see why I'm never getting married again," Amanda said. "They're all like that."

"No they aren't," Charli protested. "My dad never cheated on my mom. And Grandpa never cheated, right, Nonni?"

"Men and women, they're different," Grandma Rossi said. "A man will love you and make a home with you and raise *bambini* with you, and still he's always look-ing—and more than looking if he gets the chance. It's in their nature. A clever woman, she knows how to please her man, how to be all women to him so he doesn't stray like a dog off its leash."

Raven could only assume Grandma Rossi had been one of those clever women who knew how to keep her man on a short leash. If her adored Sergio had slipped up once or twice during their sixty-year union, she wasn't about to make it public at this late date.

Amanda said, "You're right about one thing, Mrs.

Rossi. Men are dogs." She asked Raven, "Would you like me to fire Brent for you?"

"No!"

Grandma Rossi said, "I could have his legs broken."

"*No!*"

"I was kidding!"

Sunny asked, "Don't you think Brent will settle down when things get more serious?"

"Frankly, I doubt it."

"Have you talked to him about it?" Charli asked.

"No." Raven fiddled with her napkin. "He doesn't know I know."

"Why not?" Sunny asked. "Maybe you could clear everything up."

"I'm just...not comfortable talking to him about this."

"Well, get over it," Amanda advised. "Confront the cheating cur and watch him squirm."

Raven directed her gaze to the lace tablecloth. "It's complicated."

Grandma Rossi made a humming sound—a gruff, prolonged and very knowing kind of sound.

Sunny sat back. "Uh-oh."

"You've got it all wrong!" Raven cried.

Charli's face fell. "Raven? Are you cheating on Brent?"

"No! I mean, what if I am? He cheated first."

Grandma Rossi was ready with practical advice. "Whatever you do, don't let him find out."

"Who's the lucky guy?" Amanda asked.

"There's no lucky guy," Raven insisted. "Not anymore. It's over. Not that it was ever really..." She dropped her head in her hands and groaned.

She hadn't seen Hunter in two and a half interminable weeks, since he'd treated her to his own brand of hands-on therapy, right there on the recliner reserved for her hypnosis clients.

"Well, if you still had this other guy," Sunny said, picking at her second helping of cheesecake, "and you really liked him, then maybe it would be okay to break up with Brent before the three months are up. I guess we never really thought about that."

"But she doesn't still have the other guy," Amanda said. "Come on, Raven, who is it?"

"It's not important. Just a guy I was...not even seeing, just..."

"Lusting for in your heart?" Amanda teased. Then she gasped. "It's the brother!"

The other three women gasped in unison.

Sunny said, "You're sleeping with Brent's brother?"

"I'm not sleeping with him!"

"Not anymore," Amanda said.

Grandma Rossi made that funny humming noise again, louder this time.

"I didn't sleep with him. Exactly."

Amanda drained her demitasse cup. "Exactly what kind of sex *did* you have with your boyfriend's little brother?"

Grandma Rossi asked, "Did you use a condom?"

"It wasn't like that! We just— It was— Anyway, under the circumstances, I can't keep seeing Brent."

Sunny, ever practical, asked, "Why? If this thing with Hunter is over."

"Because she doesn't want it to be over," Amanda said. "She wants the hunky little brother. She doesn't want to settle for the cheating cur."

"Even if it weren't over, it would be over," Raven said. "What I mean is, it was doomed from the start, me and Hunter. He has a very strong sense of family loyalty."

"Good boy," Grandma Rossi pronounced. "*La famiglia* is everything."

"He feels as awful as I do about what happened. Worse. Until this thing with me, he's always been very close to Brent. I feel like I've just ripped them apart."

"So even if you broke up with Brent," Charli said, "you still couldn't have Hunter because he'd feel like he's stealing you from his brother."

"And it's not just that." Raven slumped in her chair. "Hunter isn't the marrying type. He's still so young—twenty-six—and he's got these heavy responsibilities running his club. Marriage is something he won't even let himself think about. Even if it were possible for me to be with him...eventually I'd want to get married. I'd want children. The whole nine yards. It couldn't last."

Sunny sighed gustily. "Honey, I know you don't want to hear this, but you have to stick it out with Brent. Talk with him. Let him know how you feel. Maybe he just needs to know you take the relationship seriously."

"I think she's right," Charli said. "And anyway, if we start disregarding the rules this early in the pact, then the whole thing will fall apart and no one will get anything out of it."

"Stick it out for the last month," Amanda said. "If you can't make him repent, then make him suffer. I'll be happy to give you some tips."

Raven turned to Grandma Rossi for support, but all she did was shrug and jerk her head toward Amanda. "For once, I agree with this one."

"This must be why you stopped doing amateur night at Hunter's club," Sunny said.

When Raven nodded, Charli said, "I hated it that you quit. You were doing so great! Can't you go back? It's a busy place—you don't really have to deal with Hunter too much there, do you?"

"Well, not really, if I don't want to."

Raven left the rest unsaid. True, she was eager to get back onstage, but more than that, she was eager to see Hunter again—just to see him, literally. To look at him, to drink in his familiar features, to hear his rich, seductive voice. She could do that at the crowded club, without violating her resolution not to be alone with him.

Especially if...

"I'll make sure Brent is with me," she said. "If he's not there, I don't go."

Sunny shrugged. "Makes sense to me." The other women nodded their agreement.

"That's settled then. I'll find out if Brent is free on Wednesday."

Raven was already counting the hours.

12

RAVEN PAUSED in the open doorway of Hunter's tiny office, located behind the bar at Stitches. He was preoccupied, going over the paperwork for a liquor delivery with Matt, the assistant manager, and didn't notice her at first.

She hadn't been prepared for the raw, breathtaking pleasure of setting eyes on him for the first time in three weeks. His thick, dark hair curled over the collar of his black twill shirt, which was open at the neck and tucked into a pair of khaki pants. His sleeves were, as always, rolled up, and as he flipped through the pages tucked into a clipboard and gestured at items on a list, Raven observed his long fingers, his powerful wrists and forearms.

That triggered a memory of what they'd done on the recliner in her office—what *he'd* done, the way he'd touched her, the way those callused fingertips had fondled her sensitive nipples. He'd pressed his hand between her legs as she came, caressing her rhythmically, prolonging it, compelling her to surrender control and trust him.

And when she would have given him the same pleasure, he'd stopped her. Not because of a lack of desire, but to spare her further distress.

Hunter assumed her feelings for him were superficial, driven by nothing more profound than hormones. If she'd been tempted to agree before, the past three weeks had left no room for doubt. What she felt for her boyfriend's brother went far beyond any lowly chemical reaction.

And there was nothing she could do about it. Charli's summation on Sunday had been accurate. Even if Raven broke up with Brent, she still wouldn't be able to have Hunter. As much as he might desire her, family came first. That simple tenet was fundamental to his personal code of honor—and part of what made him the kind of man Raven could love.

He wouldn't jeopardize his relationship with his brother for her. It was as simple as that.

Hunter looked up and spotted her then, leaning on the doorjamb. She saw the flash of surprise before his features settled into an impenetrable mask.

Her voice was soft, almost timid. "Hi."

Matt glanced up from the papers. "Raven! I thought you'd abandoned us. Figured you were booked on Leno and Letterman and didn't need us anymore."

"What, leave my adoring fans?" she joked. "Um, is there room in the lineup for me tonight?"

"For you? We'll make room." Matt pushed his wire-rimmed glasses up his nose and consulted one of the papers on his clipboard. "How does number three sound?"

"It sounds scary. I've never been one of the first before."

"What can I tell you? You're moving up in the world."

Hunter spoke at last. "Matt, go check the sound system, okay? It cut out a couple of times last night."

"I did. It was a loose—"

"Well, double-check it."

Matt started to say something, then glanced at Raven. "Sure, no problem." He scooted past her and was gone.

Hunter perched on the edge of his cluttered steel desk, a dented relic that must have come with the place. He folded his arms. "I didn't think you were coming back here."

"Neither did I. Um, Brent's meeting me here."

She didn't have to say why. Hunter knew. She saw it in his eyes.

Raven knew she shouldn't be here, alone with Hunter in his office, even with the door standing wide open. She felt both apprehensive and titillated, like some high school kid violating curfew.

"Amanda and Charli and Sunny...they urged me to keep going onstage. They said it's good for me."

"It is," he said. "I never wanted you to stop."

He didn't smile, didn't approach her. He might have been reciting actuarial tables for all the warmth in his voice. Raven had to remind herself that this was the man who'd brought her such shattering pleasure, who'd cradled her so tenderly afterward and called her "angel."

This is how it will be between us, she thought. From now on, all her interactions with Hunter would no doubt be just like this one—stilted, formal. Even after she broke up with Brent, which she would almost certainly do next month, this invisible wall would exist between her and his brother.

The phone on his desk rang. Raven mouthed a good-bye as he answered it. She hadn't taken three steps when he called her back.

"It's for you. Brent," he said, handing her the phone and letting himself out of his office. He closed the door behind him.

"Hunter didn't have to call you to the phone," Brent said. "I told him he could take a message."

Raven said, "I thought you'd be here by now." Brent had told her he was going to the gym after work, that he'd probably make it to the club before her and grab a table.

"The damnedest thing happened. I tore my Achilles tendon working out. Hurts like hell. I guess I didn't do enough stretching."

Raven's fingers tightened around the phone receiver. She hated the direction of her thoughts; she never used to be a suspicious person. "What were you doing that tore your Achilles tendon?" she asked.

"Leg presses. I'm icing it now. The thing is, I'm not going to make it there to watch you perform tonight. I'm sorry, hon."

"Shouldn't you go to the doctor?"

"I will tomorrow if it doesn't get better. So listen, good luck, not that you'll need—"

"Is it your right leg or your left?"

"Uh, my right."

"How did you get home from the gym?"

"I drove."

"That must've been rough with your right Achilles tendon torn."

He hesitated slightly, then said, "What can I tell you? I'm tough. Listen, I gotta go lie down."

With who? she thought. "Don't forget to limp next time you see me."

Raven let the weighty silence hang there. She couldn't do this anymore, couldn't keep her mouth shut while Brent slipped around and worked his angles and patted himself on the back for being so damn good at it.

Contrary to Hunter's knee-jerk assessment, she wasn't a doormat, and she could no longer stomach acting like one. Her futile, guilt-ridden longing for Hunter had kept her from confronting Brent before now. She'd been afraid of opening up a can of worms. But it was clear that Brent no longer considered his brother a threat, if he was willing to let her perform at Stitches without his watchful presence.

Either that or the bimbo du jour was just too damn irresistible.

He said, "'Don't forget to limp?' What's that supposed to mean? You don't think I'm injured?"

"No, I don't, but even if you are, it's not what's keeping you away tonight. Is it the woman you took to Catamount on that ski weekend?"

Brent's voice betrayed a simmering fury. "What did Hunter tell you?"

"Hunter didn't have to tell me anything. I figured it out on my own, Brent. It wasn't that hard. The girl with the long black hair—is she the one who left that dog-eared issue of *Vegetarian Times* in your magazine rack?" Brent was a confirmed meat eater. "Maybe she's the same one who left her diaphragm in your medicine chest."

It sounded like Brent was switching the phone to his other ear while he formulated a response. "Raven, hon, I never wanted to hurt you."

"Oh. That must be why you lied instead of being up front and telling me from the very beginning that you don't want an exclusive relationship. 'I want us to see other people.' That's all you had to say."

"But you didn't want to see other people!"

"Okay, so let me fill in the part you're not saying. I didn't want to see other guys, which was fine with you, but you wanted to see other women, so you let me think—"

"You make it sound like I was cheating on you!"

"Excuse me?" Raven gaped at the phone. "You *were* cheating on me, Brent. That's what cheating is!"

"You weren't ready for more. You wanted to wait. I had no problem with that."

"Oh, so let me get this straight. There's nothing wrong with you sleeping with other women while you're supposedly seeing only me, because you have these raging masculine needs that have to find an outlet or you'll, I don't know, have major organ failure or something—"

"Oh, please," he muttered.

"—so while you're waiting for me to decide I'm ready for intimacy, it's perfectly all right to lie and cheat and cover it up."

After a few moments, Brent said, "If you'd given me some indication that you were really and truly committed to me, I wouldn't have done it."

"Don't you dare try to put the blame for your actions on me! I told you two months ago I was seeing only you. On several occasions we discussed the seriousness of our relationship. For a while I thought it might lead to something permanent."

He sounded subdued. "And now?"

"It's over." At this point, not even the Wedding Ring pact could keep her plodding along in this blighted relationship.

"Don't do that, Raven. Let's talk about this."

"There's no point in dragging it out, Brent. My mind is made up."

"I made a mistake. Don't throw away what we have over one mistake. It's not how things will be in the future. I swear."

"Brent—"

"Look, I'm coming to the club. I'll be there in—"

"No. Don't come here."

"We have to talk."

"Not tonight. Not here. I don't want to see you right now, Brent."

Just then Raven heard, over the phone line, the sound of a door opening, followed by a feminine voice raised in question. She couldn't make out Brent's muffled response—obviously he'd clapped his hand over the mouthpiece—but she did hear the door close firmly. Then he was back, sounding rattled.

"Tomorrow night, Raven. I'll come to your place."

"I'm going to a movie with Amanda tomorrow. Brent, please, we have nothing to talk—"

"Friday, then."

It was clear he wasn't going to yield on this. Raven figured it wouldn't hurt to see him one last time. She'd hear him out, give him a chance to explain his actions, though she knew that nothing he could say at this point would sway her. After he'd had his say, she would officially break up with him.

That was the right way to do it. Cheating or no cheating, after a two-month relationship, he was entitled to hear it in person.

"All right," she said. "Friday evening."

"I'll come over at—"

"No. I'll come to your place," Raven said. It would give her more control—she could leave whenever she wanted.

"My place, then. Come around seven. I'll make dinner."

"No dinner."

"Raven—"

"This isn't a date, Brent. Let's just concentrate on clearing the air."

"All right. Friday at seven. We'll get past this, Raven," he promised. "We'll work it out. You'll see."

After she hung up, Raven was in no mood to get a table for one and order dinner. She sat in the bar nursing a nonalcoholic bloody Mary and chatting with the bartender, Yvonne, until the show started.

She was a little nervous, having been away from the stage for several weeks, but once she walked out under the lights, it didn't take her long to get up to speed. Her routine centered around a recent trip to Fort Lauderdale to visit her retired parents. She capitalized on generational differences that she knew most of her audience could identify with, and the crowd rewarded her with raucous applause.

After her act, Raven was invited by a couple of other regulars she was friendly with to join them at their table and take in the rest of the show. Now that her act was over, she allowed herself a real bloody Mary. The drink was strong, her stomach was empty and it didn't take long to feel a warm glow from the vodka.

Raven waited impatiently for each amateur routine to conclude, at which time Hunter would stride onstage and introduce the next act. Onstage he was witty and relaxed and, more than anything, himself. A far cry from the chilly reserve he'd treated her to earlier.

I have to do something about this, Raven thought. It didn't have to be like that between them.

She brooded over her predicament until a zaftig, sixtyish woman named Dolores Beal claimed the stage. Dolores had a no-nonsense look about her that commanded respect, despite her blindingly multihued pantsuit and her retro hairdo, teased to the max. Her hair was a uniform dark chestnut except for a startling streak of white at the browline. The Bride of Frankenstein's wisecracking sister.

"I'm a victim," Dolores began, deadpan. She went on to explain that she was victimized by her addiction to Circus Peanuts, those soft, orange, peanut-shaped candies sold for Halloween. Her shameful habit had led her to filch the stuff from her grandkids' trick-or-treat bags, but it was never enough, and she inevitably went into withdrawal around Thanksgiving. She tried to ease her cravings with candy corn, but it just wasn't the same.

If Raven was adept at timing, Dolores was a master. Her act was interspersed with weighty pauses during which she stared straight-faced at her audience as they succumbed to ever-increasing hilarity.

Her satirical routine focused on the popular tendency to attribute people's bad behavior to forces beyond their control. She named a married public official renowned for his sexual hijinks. Not his fault. The poor man was addicted to sex; *Hard Copy* said so. That teenager in the news, the one who murdered his parents? Mommy and Daddy made him rake the leaves. Who wouldn't snap after that kind of abuse?

Raven found herself engrossed in the funny, insightful routine. Dolores spoke of a zillionaire rock star currently being lauded by the media for his "courageous" battle with his tragic cocaine addiction. She cracked up the whole room even as she drove home the importance of personal responsibility.

Eventually the show ended and Hunter sent the crowd on their way. The club emptied out except for the staff cleaning up and shutting the place down.

Raven found Hunter in his office, but he wasn't alone. He stood chatting with an attractive older couple and Dolores Beal, who'd planted herself in his desk chair.

"Oh, I'll, uh, catch you later," Raven mumbled, backing out of the room.

"You're not going anywhere," Dolores said. "We were about to send Hunter out after you."

"Me?"

The other woman approached Raven and seized her hands, smiling warmly. "We've been dying to meet you, Raven. Brent has told us so much about you. I'm Audrey Radley and this is my husband, Mike."

Brent and Hunter's parents! Raven shot a glance at Hunter, whose stolid mask was now firmly in place.

"It's...great to meet you," she said. "Um, Brent said you were in England the last few weeks. Visiting relatives."

"We just got back yesterday." Mike Radley pumped her hand. "Brent told us you were as talented as you are beautiful, and he wasn't lying. You were very funny up there."

"I give you a lot of credit for being able to do that," Audrey said. "It must be very intimidating."

"Where *is* that fella of yours, by the way?" Mike asked. "He told us he'd be here tonight."

"Brent couldn't make it," Raven said. "He tore his Achilles tendon at the gym."

Audrey frowned. "I spoke to him after he got home. He never said anything about an injury."

Raven caught Hunter's eye. That telltale muscle twitched in his jaw and he looked away.

"Well, maybe he didn't want to worry you," Raven said. "I got the feeling it wasn't that serious."

"So when are you and Brent coming to dinner?" Mike boomed, and turned to his wife. "How about Sunday! We'll make a ham."

"Great!" Audrey seconded.

"Oh, I—I don't know," Raven hedged. "Actually, I believe I have something planned for Sunday."

Like being their son's *ex*-girlfriend by then. She certainly wasn't about to let Brent's family in on her plans to break up with him in two days. Not even Brent deserved that kind of disrespect.

"How about next Sunday, then?" Audrey asked.

"Uh..."

Dolores said, "Back off a little, Audrey. Let the girl catch her breath."

"You were wonderful out there," Raven told Dolores, eager to change the subject.

"Thanks. These two talked me into it," she said, gesturing to Audrey and Mike.

"So how does it compare to the pulpit?" Hunter asked.

"I couldn't be sure with those lights in my eyes, but I don't think anyone dozed off on me."

Mike said, "No one dozes during your sermons, Dolores. They wouldn't dare."

"Sermons?" Raven said, wide-eyed. "No wonder you seemed like a natural up there. You're a ringer!"

Hunter cracked a smile at last. "Raven, I'd like you to meet Reverend Dolores Beal, of the North Shore Unitarian Church."

Dolores scowled at him. "Oh, so you remember what it's called, at least. When did you graduate religious school, Hunter? Ten, eleven years ago?"

"Thirteen," he admitted.

"Thirteen years! How many times have you set foot in the church in the last thirteen years?"

Hunter looked to his parents for support. His father raised his hands as if to say, *You're on your own, Son.*

"I'm running a business!" Hunter said. "It's not that easy to get up on Sunday mornings after three hours sleep—"

"That lame excuse only covers the last couple of years. And anyway, if you're such a crackerjack businessman, we could use you on the ways and means committee. That's one Tuesday night a month. And bring that wayward brother of yours." Dolores addressed Raven as she hauled herself to her feet. "Unless Brent's worshiping somewhere else nowadays?"

Raven met her stare for a few seconds before the significance of the question sank in. "Oh! No, we're not—Brent and I don't worsh— I mean, that's not how we spend our Sunday mornings."

Hunter's parents chuckled knowingly. Even Reverend Beal couldn't suppress an indulgent smile. Only Hunter appeared unamused.

That's not what I meant! Raven felt her face flame.

"No comment," Dolores said. "Hunter, I have to say, you've done a terrific job with this place. I'm proud of you." She patted his cheek. "I had fun tonight."

"Come back anytime, Reverend. The crowd loves you."

"We have to get going." Audrey hugged Raven, her eyes brimming with genuine affection. "Make Brent bring you around. Soon, okay?"

Raven groped for a response and settled for, "I'm so glad we got to meet at last."

Dolores and the Radleys left. Halfway out the door himself, Hunter said, "I've got to count the receipts, Raven. What did you want to see me about?"

"We need to talk." Raven fiddled with one of the horn buttons closing her mandarin-collared ivory tunic. Um...I guess this isn't a good time."

"No, it's not."

She searched his rigid features, seeking some shred of the warmth she knew was under the surface. It had to be. No one could turn his feelings off like a light switch.

"I'll wait," she said. "I'm not in any hurry."

Hunter looked away for a moment, then back at her. "We don't have anything to talk about."

The words were like a slap. Wasn't that what she'd told Brent earlier that evening?

Raven struggled for composure as she said, "I think we do."

For an instant, as she looked into his eyes, she detected a silent plea. *Leave it alone. Don't make this harder than it has to be.* Then the mask was back and he turned away with an abrupt, "Suit yourself."

13

HUNTER TOOK HIS TIME counting the receipts and battening down the hatches, hoping Raven would lose patience and leave. Instead she parked herself on the edge of the stage, sitting cross-legged, her long, plum-colored skirt draped demurely over her knees.

And waited.

When the last of his staff departed, Hunter lingered in the storeroom, spending twenty minutes rearranging boxes and double-checking paper supplies. He wasted another ten minutes fine-tuning payroll spreadsheets on the computer, and twenty more inventorying china and glassware. Eventually he had no choice but to reenter the club, brightly lit now that the overhead fixtures had been turned on.

The room looked more than a little shabby under the harsh fluorescent glare, like a venerable grand dame stepping out of the flattering shadows into unforgiving sunlight. Chairs were upended on the battered tables, now stripped of their homey tablecloths. The dark paneling, installed decades ago when this building was a family-style Italian restaurant, was gouged and pocked with nail holes. The black and white floor tiles, still damp from their nightly scrubbing, were cracked and scored. The acrid odor of powerful cleaning agents hung heavy in the air. Hunter was a little embarrassed to have Raven see the place like this.

She looked up from the newspaper she'd no doubt swiped from his office, and asked pleasantly, "Done already? Doesn't the flatware need to be polished? Maybe you should count the martini olives, make sure you have enough for the next year and a half."

Hunter swung a chair off the table nearest her and sat backward on it, propping his forearms on the chairback. The speakers had long since been turned off; the only background music now was the faint drumroll of a late winter rainstorm pummeling the building's flat roof.

He said, "I seem to recall you saying something about never being alone with me again."

She looked so young and fresh, sitting cross-legged on the scarred wooden stage, the newspaper spread out on her lap, her shoulder bag and greenish-gray trench coat lying near her in a heap.

She folded the paper and set it aside. "It doesn't have to be like this, Hunter." He started to reply, but she cut him off. "And don't tell me you don't know what I'm talking about. You're so cold and distant, you'd think I did something terrible to you."

"You don't think you're overstating it just a bit?"

"No, I don't."

"Raven." He rested his chin on his folded arms and regarded her levelly. "What do you want?"

She raised her hands, let them fall. "I just want things

to be like they used to be between us. Simple. Natural. Is that too much to ask?"

He gave her a grim half smile. "Things have never been simple between us, and doing what comes naturally isn't an option under the circumstances."

"So we have to walk on eggs around each other from now on, is that it?"

"That's it," he said.

She waited. He stared back stoically. What did she want him to do, soften the truth by pretending they could have some chummy, platonic, in-law-type relationship?

In a small voice she said, "If this is how it has to be, I wish I hadn't come back here. I should've listened to my gut and stayed away."

"What would that accomplish? We'll still have to see each other, because of Brent, still have to deal with each other."

She hesitated. "And if Brent were no longer in the picture?"

"What do you mean?" Hunter straightened. "You're not breaking up with him."

She started to respond, but her words died on a frustrated sigh.

"If you were going to end it with Brent," he said, "you'd have done it when you first found out he was messing around. And if you're thinking of dumping him now because you've got a case of the hots for his kid brother, think again, because I won't have you," he added with brutal candor. "You've got to know I'd never do that to family."

The color had leached from Raven's face. Her voice quavered. "I know that."

Hunter hated doing this to her, but he couldn't allow her to think she could discard his brother to pursue a fling with him. Brent was still family—and Raven was obviously devoted to him, to have patiently waited out his alley-catting for this long. She'd invested two months of her life in a relationship that was clearly headed toward the altar. Neither she nor Brent had made a secret of their desire to settle down.

Hunter wouldn't be doing Raven any favors, either, if he let her squander her future with Brent for a fleeting affair with him. He'd told her way back during that first double date that he wasn't the marrying type, and if his feelings on the issue had become somewhat muddled during the past two months, she didn't need to know that. As far as she was concerned, he was still a poster boy for happy-go-lucky bachelorhood, and her boyfriend's brother to boot—which made him doubly off-limits. Which might help explain her physical attraction to him: the allure of the unattainable.

He only wished his feelings for her were that uncomplicated.

He said, "Are you sleeping with him yet?" He hadn't intended to ask, but that remark about how they spent their Sunday mornings had been plaguing him.

After a moment she said, "No."

"Have you thought that if you spread your legs for your man, he might stop screwing around?"

Never before had Raven looked at Hunter like this, as if taking his measure and finding him lacking. His fingers gripped the chairback so hard they cramped.

Quietly she asked, "Are you trying to make me hate you?"

Is it working? "Maybe you're waiting for the wedding night. Brent said you're an old-fashioned girl."

"You'd be very happy if I followed your example and pretended I feel nothing for you. I can't do it, Hunter. I won't do it."

"How goddamn naive are you?" He sprang to his feet, toppling the chair. "You're *going* to follow my example because anything else is pointless and destructive!"

Raven scooted off the stage and stalked right up to him. "Is this pointless and destructive?" She pulled his head down and kissed him on the mouth.

Hunter exulted in the gut-deep pleasure of it, for a stunned instant, before his internal censor categorized this as a dangerous activity. Then he responded without forethought, shoving Raven away, hard. She stumbled backward and collided with the edge of the stage.

Conflicting impulses assailed him for the scant seconds it took her to catch her breath. The next thing he knew, she'd snatched up her bag and coat and bolted from the room.

Every muscle tensed to tear out after her. *Let her go,*

that internal censor commanded, as the club's outer door banged shut. *This is what you want.*

No, not what he wanted, Hunter thought, but what he needed, what they both needed: a yawning chasm between them, too vast for either to leap.

He scrubbed his hands over his face, but he couldn't scrub away the taste of her, the phantom touch of her lips.

With a raw curse he sprinted through the club and out the back door, into the dark parking lot. Needles of freezing rain soaked him to the skin; his breath smoked like a locomotive in the downpour. The pole-mounted security light showed that the lot was empty except for Hunter's dark green Outback, in the far corner, and Raven's gray Mazda sedan, now racing toward the exit.

Hunter was beyond rational thought. He charged the car, throwing himself at the front of it as the vehicle skidded to a squealing stop on the rain-battered blacktop. The overworked wipers revealed Raven's startled face in fleeting bursts, her knuckles white on the wheel.

He lunged for the passenger door handle, only to hear the locks engage with an audible *chunk* just before he reached it. He yanked hard on the handle, to no avail. "Open the door, Raven!" He slammed his fist on the window glass. *"Open it!"*

"Leave me alone!" she screamed, and started to pull away.

Taking a running vault, Hunter swung his right leg onto the hood, boosting himself fully onto it. She braked hard again, sending him sliding off the car. He scrambled back onto it and stared through the windshield at her rigid features as icy rain hammered him like buckshot.

"Unlock this car, Raven!"

She responded with a ripe oath. If he had to stay out here all night, in this bitter torrent, he would. She must have known it, because after a lengthy stare-down, she unlocked the car.

Hunter leaped off the hood and jerked the door open. He folded himself into the front passenger seat and slammed the door shut. He was drenched to the bone, his black shirt and khaki pants plastered to his body, soaking the velour upholstery. Raven wasn't much drier, having fled the club without taking time to put her coat on. She trembled, from outrage as much as the cold, he suspected. He was still too pumped with adrenaline to feel much of anything at the moment.

Little light made it through the pounding rain that shrouded the window glass, even less when Hunter reached over and killed the engine, halting the wipers in midswipe. He slipped Raven's car keys into his pants pocket.

"I didn't mean to do that," he said tightly. "To shove you like I did in there. I don't know where that came from. I would never—" He thrust his wet hair off his forehead. "I'm sorry as hell, Raven. That's all I can tell you."

Raven listened stoically, her gaze directed at the fogged windshield and the impenetrable downpour beyond. Her hair lay in sodden strands around her face. She shivered violently now.

"Put this on," he said, reaching into the back seat for her trench coat. He pushed her right arm into the sleeve as she struggled into the coat, tugging the front closed without buttoning it.

And still she didn't look at him. She'd wait him out, he knew, just as she'd done earlier inside the club. Only this time, all she wanted was for him to leave her be. So she could go home, lick her emotional wounds and shore up her defenses against him.

It's what you need, what you demanded of her, he reminded himself. *Give her her keys, let her go.*

"Say something," he said. "I'm not going to leave until you tell me what you're thinking."

She shut her eyes, pulled the coat tighter around her.

"Do you hate me?" he asked.

"Isn't that what you wanted?"

"Yes," he whispered.

"I wish I could," she choked out on a sob. "I wish I could hate you. It's so easy for you."

His throat constricted. "Is that what you think? That I hate you?" He reached for her. She jerked away, but he caught her by the upper arms and hauled her across the space between the bucket seats, awkwardly settling her on his lap with her booted feet on the driver's seat.

"I don't hate you, angel." He wiped the wet hair off her cold cheeks, her forehead. "God, how could I ever hate you? Look at me."

He tipped her face toward his, but her eyes were

closed once more as she silently wept. "I don't know how to get us past this," he confessed, "and that's why I'm saying all the wrong things, and doing all the wrong things. I don't know how to be with you and not want you. How could I ever stop wanting you?"

He kissed her eyes, tasted the salt of her tears. "Look at me," he insisted, and she did, and what he saw in her eyes cut through his defenses like a scalpel. On some level he knew it was more than lust he saw in those gilded depths, more than animal attraction, even as he denied it, even as he captured her mouth in a fierce, deep kiss.

She still clutched her coat closed like a shield. He seized her wrist and pulled her arm away, slid his hand inside the coat and over the damp front of her tunic. She shuddered and tried to draw back, but he soothed her with his endless kiss and the tender urgency of his touch.

Her breast filled his hand, warm and pliant, the nipple stiff against his palm, inflaming him. Raven's breathing quickened as he caressed her with growing hunger. The cold bit through his wet clothes now, but she was in his arms, and his senses fed on her, on the fragrant, supple heat of her.

At some point he stopped thinking, let the untamed part of him slip its leash. Instinct guided his hand up her calf, under the hem of her skirt and higher, seeking. Her silky stocking ended in a garterlike band at mid-thigh and then there was only the scorching silk of her skin.

They both groaned as his fingers splayed over the bare top of her thigh. Raven was kissing him back now, greedily plucking at his lips as her arms wound around his neck. Her thighs parted slightly; he doubted she was aware of it. The simple, spontaneous movement propelled him off a precipice he'd been teetering on for two long months.

Hunter slid his hand between her legs, over the thin cotton of her underpants. He felt the shape of her through the cloth and the springy curls, traced her womanly furrow with a fingertip. Her breath caught. She went very still.

He eased his fingers under the leg opening and touched her slippery folds. Raven gasped his name. Her nails dug into his shoulders even as her legs parted further in unconscious invitation.

"That's it, angel." One finger found her narrow opening and pushed into her. "Oh, you're beautiful...yes..." he murmured, burrowing deeper into the sleek, snug heat of her.

"Hunter..." she whimpered, whether in passion or distress, he couldn't say.

"Shh." He quieted her with a kiss.

As her hips rocked in cadence with his thrusting finger, her bottom ground against his aching erection, snapping the fragile thread of his control. Withdrawing his hand, he wrenched her underpants down her legs and over her ankle boots, ripping the flimsy fabric in the process. His movements were quick now, almost rough; he was deaf to his internal censor, too far gone for second thoughts.

He brought her left leg over his hips so that she straddled him, even as he unzipped his pants and released his engorged penis. Holding Raven steady, he rammed into her hard and fast. Her short, piercing scream reverberated in the confines of the car. She was tight, mind-numbingly tight. Pulling her against him, he forced himself higher, deeper, as a guttural sound rumbled up his throat.

Her inner muscles gripped him, goaded him. He responded with a savage thrust, and another. His fingers bit into her flesh as he raised and lowered her on his pumping hips, mindlessly seeking the merciful oblivion of release. That release came with such guilt-driven haste that Raven never had a chance to reach her own climax.

But even in the grip of his blinding orgasm, even as he emptied himself into her, his shame was stamped so deeply on his soul that it seared him like a brand. He was left spent and winded, consumed by self-loathing, unable to face the woman he loved.

The humid, musky warmth inside the car was suddenly suffocating. Gently Hunter lifted Raven off him. He zipped his pants and dropped her car keys on the dash, and let himself out into the stinging downpour.

14

THE POUNDING DIDN'T WAKE Hunter. He was already wide-awake, having spent a second sleepless night wondering how he would ever be able to face his brother again. The booming voice on the other side of his apartment door told him he was about to find out.

"Hunter, let me in, damn it!" The pounding increased: *bang! bang! bang!*

Hunter glanced at his wrist, only to find it bare. The morning TV talk shows he'd been listlessly channel surfing had been on for about half an hour, so he figured it must be around seven-thirty.

Brent knew Hunter usually slept until at least ten, after getting home from the club 2:00 a.m. on weekdays. The list of what could have brought Brent to his brother's door at seven-thirty in the morning was woefully short. Either someone had died or—

Bang! Bang! Bang! Bang! Bang!

"Open up!"

Raven had told him.

Mrs. Flynn from across the hall hollered at Brent to knock it off, people were trying to sleep. Hunter clicked the TV off with the remote control, abandoned the sofa where he'd been sprawled and padded barefoot to the front door, clad in an undershirt and navy sweatpants.

As he unlocked the door, his entire body tensed in anticipation—an automatic fight-or-flight response that was superfluous in this case, considering that he had no intention of doing either. If Brent had come here to mete out punishment for his kid brother's monumental act of betrayal, then the kid brother would damn well stand there and take it like a man.

Hunter paused for a moment with his hand on the doorknob. He took a breath, let it out, swung open the door.

And flew backward as the heel of Brent's hand rammed his shoulder. He staggered and steadied himself, his fingers reflexively curling into fists despite his grim resolve to let his brother beat the hell out of him.

"I bet you thought this day would never come!" Brent roared, kicking the door shut with a flourish.

Hunter backed up a step or two, rubbing his shoulder, trying to decipher the peculiar euphoric look on his brother's face. Was he drunk?

Or simply relishing the anticipation?

Brent advanced on him, that maniacal grin still pasted on his face. "Ask me why I'm here." He shoved Hunter again. "Ask me what was so important I had to come here and roust you out of bed." Another shove, till Hunter was backed against the coffee table. "Go ahead, ask me."

He's lost it, Hunter thought. *He's gone over the edge. And I put him there.*

Brent waited, eager and bright-eyed, for Hunter to play along and ask.

"Uh...okay," Hunter said at last. "What brings you here?"

Brent's hand darted into the breast pocket of his brown leather bomber jacket. Hunter's arms jerked up in a defensive gesture, much to his brother's amusement.

"You always so jumpy when you don't get your beauty rest?" Brent asked. "Speaking of which, I don't mind telling you, you look like hell, Bro."

Hunter was only half listening. He was staring at what Brent had taken out of his pocket. A tiny box clad in burgundy velvet.

A ring box.

Hunter's sleep-deprived mind debated whether he might at this moment be dreaming, as Brent held the box in front of his face and opened it. A hefty diamond winked from its nest of white satin, a classic round-cut stone perched in an equally classic yellow gold setting.

"An old-fashioned ring for an old-fashioned girl," Brent proclaimed.

An old-fashioned girl. "You bought this for Raven?"

"Who else, Bro? Think she'll like it?" Brent peered closely at the ring. "The guy said I could bring it back and pick one out with her, but I'm pretty sure she'll go for this one."

Brent didn't know, then. Raven hadn't told him. She'd had all yesterday to do it, to confess to Brent about what had happened in her car in the parking lot behind Stitches, and she'd chosen not to.

And now Brent had bought an engagement ring for his old-fashioned girlfriend.

Six weeks has passed since Hunter's "if I'd met her first" admission. Brent's initial ire had gradually cooled off, and just last week he'd offered an awkward apology to Hunter for having flown off the handle. He'd made a couple of lame jokes about lusting after most of Hunter's girlfriends, and had assured him that he trusted him. At that point, after not having laid eyes on Raven for over two weeks, Hunter almost believed himself worthy of that trust.

"She's coming over tonight," Brent said, snapping the box shut and tucking it back into his jacket. "Twelve hours from now, I'll be an engaged man. Too late for you to steal her away from me." Chuckling, he aimed a mock one-two punch at Hunter's midsection. Hunter flinched, his abs tightening painfully, though Brent's fists never made contact.

"Hey, you really *are* jumpy." Brent slapped him on the shoulder. "Listen, go back to bed. I'm on my way to an early meeting at the magazine. Just wanted to drop by and give you the good news." He turned to let himself out.

"How do you know she'll say yes?"

Brent spun back toward him. "What? Of course she'll say yes. What do you think she's been waiting for all this time?"

Two months didn't seem like "all this time" to

Hunter, but he supposed to truly marriage-minded people in their thirties, it might constitute a long-term relationship.

Hunter had intended to confess all to Brent, as soon he could figure out a way to say it. Part of him wanted to blurt it out now, to exorcize it, to take this crushing burden of guilt and catapult it into the open. The admission wouldn't alleviate his shame, but it would provide a much-needed catharsis.

But what would it do to Brent? And Raven? What had happened between Hunter and Raven was his fault, not hers. Not that she hadn't been willing, but he was the one who'd gone after her when she'd tried to leave, he was the one who'd bullied his way into her car. He'd taken advantage of her emotional vulnerability and her physical attraction to him, exploiting them for his own gratification.

Certainly not for hers. He'd used her roughly, and left her unsatisfied. Hunter had always prided himself on being an unselfish lover; he'd always taken pains to pleasure his bed partner thoroughly—and safely, never forgetting to use a condom. But what had he done to the only woman he'd ever loved? Given her the wham-bam treatment and run off without a word.

And now he had to decide whether to tell Brent—the brother who'd practically raised him, the brother whose generosity had made Hunter's dream of owning his own club a reality—that he'd seduced the woman Brent adored enough to marry.

That adoration went both ways: Raven was in love

with Brent. Did Hunter have the heart to destroy their future together? Because that would surely be the result if he unburdened himself to his brother now. If Raven had made the decision not to tell Brent, did Hunter have the right to override that decision?

He had no doubt she was suffering the same guilty anguish as he, possibly even more. Of course, if one considered the fact that Brent had been cheating on her from day one, it could be argued that she had nothing to feel guilty about. Not that she'd see it that way, Hunter knew.

He hoped for Raven's sake that she wasn't pregnant—though the prospect of seeing her grow round with his child brought a stab of longing that took his breath away.

Hunter would marry her if he could. He'd bind her to him with his ring and his seed and the constancy of his love, and she'd be his forever.

Brent grimaced. "The only thing is, Raven found out about Marina. She gave me hell about it Wednesday, when I called her at the club."

Hunter said nothing. He could have told Brent she knew weeks ago.

"I was careless," Brent said. "I didn't cover my tracks well enough and Raven got hurt. I feel shitty about that, but at least now I know she really cares. So to answer your question, yeah, she'll say yes." He patted his chest pocket, where the ring resided. "And anyway, a rock like this can help smooth over a lot of hurt feelings."

Would Brent be a faithful husband? Hunter supposed anything was possible. Brent probably believed he'd been reformed by the love of a good woman, but only time would tell. Hunter hoped to God his brother had gotten his priorities straightened out. Raven deserved a husband who returned her love and fidelity in full measure.

"You've been seeing a lot of Marina," Hunter said.

Brent shrugged, but Hunter was watching his eyes, and they told an interesting story. Now that he thought about it, Hunter was pretty sure Brent hadn't fooled around with any other women after he met Marina. It would seem he'd been cheating on Raven *only* with the vegetarian, miniature-collecting swimsuit model.

Was there such a thing as monogamous infidelity?

"Didn't you tell me you were only going to see her a couple of times?" Hunter persisted.

"It doesn't matter," Brent said. "That's over. It was fun while it lasted, but you know I'm looking for something permanent."

"What, Marina's not interested in something permanent?"

"She's not marriage material," Brent said flatly.

"What does that mean, not marriage material?"

"You know what I mean."

"No, I really don't. Is she too shallow for you, is that it? A little on the vacuous side?"

Brent snapped, "You're just saying that because she's a model and she's gorgeous. The typical narrow-minded attitude. It just so happens she's got a lot up here." He tapped his head. "There are depths to Marina you couldn't begin to imagine. She's sensitive and free-thinking and— Did you know she's going for a career in holistic medicine? She knows her modeling days are numbered—she's planning ahead."

"Really."

"That's right." Brent's brisk nod said, *So there.*

Hunter couldn't recall the last time his brother had been so passionately defensive about anything. "Bear with me, I'm kinda slow," he said. "This gorgeous, smart, sensitive, farsighted woman isn't marriage material. *Why?*"

Brent gave him a pointed look. "Would you marry a girl who let you into her pants on the first date?"

Hunter was dumbfounded. "If I loved her? Why not?"

"How do I know how many other guys came before me? Marina's been around."

"Unlike you, who've lived the life of a monk, saving yourself for your wedding night—"

"You know what? If you don't know what I'm talking about, there's no use having this discussion."

"You're talking about holding Marina to a double standard."

An unpleasant bark of laughter erupted from Brent. He spread his hands, glancing around the cluttered living room. "Hey, Bro, I don't see any women around here to impress with that politically correct crap, so why don't you give it a rest."

Hunter avoided Brent's eyes as he said, "So Raven's this paragon of virtue and innocence, is that it?"

"Hey, I know she's no thirty-year-old virgin. I'm not delusional. But I also know she doesn't jump in the sack with every Tom, Dick and Harry. I don't have to worry about who she's screwing behind my back, that's for damn sure."

Suddenly Hunter was back in that gray Mazda in the parking lot behind Stitches, with the fogged windows and the drumming rain and Raven's hoarse cries as he ejaculated deep inside her.

I don't have to worry about who she's screwing behind my back.

Hunter's guilt was an anvil, crushing his chest, stealing his air. Through sheer force of will he made himself focus on the discussion. "Is that what this is about?" he asked. "Was Marina sleeping with other guys while she was seeing you?"

"Hell no!"

Hunter wanted to say, *Then what does it matter how many came before you if she's all yours now?* But he knew there were plenty of men, Brent included, who couldn't ignore the primitive male instinct that said it mattered a lot. Hunter asked, "How did she react when you called it quits?"

He saw it in his eyes even before Brent said, "I haven't, yet. Soon. I don't want to do it over the phone."

"Does she know about Raven?"

"Nah. Why invite trouble?"

"So as far as Marina knows," Hunter said, "she's the only woman in your life. Is she serious about you?"

Brent looked at his watch. "Listen, I'd love to hang out here and discuss my sex life—"

"Did you know Mom and Dad did it on their first date?"

Brent gaped at him. "Shut your lying—"

"Dad let that one slip a couple of months ago when we were tossing back a few at O'Leary's. He said the two of them were like rabbits."

"You're so full of it." Angry color suffused Brent's face. "Mom would never have done that!"

"Oh, I forgot. She was a virgin bride and has forced herself to have intercourse precisely three times, purely for the purpose of procreation."

Brent scowled. "What're you trying to do, talk me out of marrying Raven?"

Was he? Hunter thrust his fingers through his disheveled hair. "Look. I can tell you have strong feelings for Marina. I just don't want you to make a decision you'll regret later."

"Well, don't worry about me, Bro." There was a hard, determined look in Brent's eyes. "I've thought this through, examined it from all angles. Raven's the logical choice."

Since when did logic have anything to do with love?

At the door, Brent turned back, and at that moment Hunter saw not the swaggering, self-confident role model of his youth, but a guy just like him—fallible, prey to self-doubt, struggling to make the right choices.

"I need your support in this," Brent said quietly, looking him in the eye. "I need your blessing, Hunter."

Searing emotion surged within Hunter, closing his throat, stealing his voice. He reached his brother in two long strides and wrapped his arms around him. Brent hugged him back with rib-cracking force, the bond that connected them too strong for words.

"You've got it." Hunter's voice was a hoarse whisper. *Forgive me,* he silently pleaded. *Please forgive me, Brent.* "You've got my blessing."

15

SAVORY AROMAS GREETED Raven as Brent welcomed her into his house. The lights were dim; a romantic Tony Bennett CD played softly in the background—Brent knew she liked Tony Bennett. Glancing toward the dining area, she saw that the table had been set for two, complete with a cluster of round, iridescent blue-green candles floating on water in a shallow bowl of the same color.

It would seem Hunter hadn't yet told Brent about what had happened Wednesday night in her car behind Stitches.

Raven sighed. "Brent, I told you, no dinner."

"It's white lasagne," he said, taking her coat and hanging it in his front closet. "Northern Italian style. I don't think you've ever had my white lasagne. Ham, three kinds of cheese, an incredibly rich cream sauce—guaranteed to raise your cholesterol count twenty points."

He was unaccountably chipper, considering that she'd made no secret of her intention to end their relationship. Was this some kind of last-ditch effort to change her mind?

Returning to her, Brent planted a light kiss on her

mouth. He smelled good, his usual clean scent overlaid with a hint of woodsy aftershave. His smooth jaw told her he'd shaved off his five-o'clock shadow for her. The ribbed, white cotton sweater he wore displayed his wide shoulders to advantage.

Raven found herself impressed anew by this man's sheer masculine appeal, which she had to admit went beyond the physical. She could see why her matchmaking pals had considered him a catch. If it weren't for his womanizing, she might have agreed.

And if it weren't for Hunter, would she have given Brent a chance in spite of the womanizing?

No. What she'd told Grandma Rossi was the truth—she wouldn't marry a man she couldn't trust.

"Brent, I wish you hadn't done all this," she said, as he steered her toward the brick-red sofa. "I came here to clear the air—I'm not staying long."

"Why should we go hungry? You know I love to cook for you."

For me and how many others? she thought, recalling that copy of *Vegetarian Times* she'd spied in his magazine rack, and wondering if he'd begun adding non-meat dishes to his culinary repertoire.

He'd placed an assortment of Mediterranean spreads with pita triangles on the coffee table, along with two cut-crystal glasses of red wine. He handed her a wineglass. She set it back on the table.

"Brent, you can't just gloss over this whole thing. A romantic dinner isn't going to make everything right."

He sipped from his glass and set it next to hers. Taking both her hands in his, he said, "Honey, I'm not trying to gloss over anything. I'm just trying to show you how much you mean to me. I took you for granted—that's the truth and there's no way to soft-pedal it."

He gazed at her with warm sincerity, squeezing her hands. "I can tell you that it will never happen again. That's a promise. I never had anyone like you in my life before, Raven. I guess it just took this close scrape to really make me appreciate you."

"Close scrape?"

"Almost losing you."

She pulled her hands out of his grasp. "Brent—"

"Mom and Dad adore you," he said, beaming. "They told me about meeting you at Stitches on Wednesday. They're eager to get together with us—I told them tomorrow's good for brunch at their place."

"What? They're expecting us tomorrow?"

His smile broadened into a buoyant grin. "I know I won't be able to wait any longer than that to give them the good news."

"The good...?" Raven watched as Brent slipped his hand between the sofa cushions and produced a small object that looked suspiciously like a ring box.

He opened the box, revealing a traditional diamond engagement ring. The large, round-cut stone seemed to capture the room's meager light and throw it off in a blaze of sparks. "Will you marry me, Raven?"

She was struck mute as Brent lifted her left hand and slid the ring onto her finger.

"It fits," he said with a breathless chuckle, turning

her hand this way and that. "I was afraid I'd have to get it sized." He looked at her. "It looks just right on your hand, honey. Say yes. I promise, I'll make you happy. Or die trying."

The words tangled on Raven's tongue; nothing came out but a strangled sob. She covered her mouth, struggling to compose herself. How had everything gotten so turned around?

Brent dipped his head to peer at her face, his expression a mixture of concern and cautious optimism. "Dare I hope those are tears of joy?" he asked, lifting a paper napkin from the table to gently blot her eyes.

With trembling fingers she pulled the ring off.

"Raven, don't," he said, staying her hand. "Don't say no. Give us a chance—"

"It isn't meant to be." She pressed the ring into his palm.

He stared at it, closed his fist around it. "You hate me."

"I don't hate you, Brent. It just could never work out for us. There's too much...in the way."

"This thing with Marina—it didn't mean anything, it'll never happen again. What you and I have is too precious to throw away. Just think about it—that's all I ask. Give it a few days."

"Marina?"

He hesitated. "That's her name."

"I thought... Aren't there others?"

"Other women? Well, not since...I mean, once I started seeing Marina..." He sighed raggedly. "Look,

Raven, it's over, she's history, that's all that matters at this point."

"Is Marina the one you're building the dollhouse for?"

His eyes widened. "How do you know about the dollhouse?"

"Don't you remember when you sent me down to the basement to fetch those pecans from the Deepfreeze?"

"Oh..." he groaned.

"I saw this half-built dollhouse on your workbench. Brent, you don't have any nieces, no young cousins I'm aware of. And that Victorian villa down there is so exquisitely detailed, with that delicate gingerbread and those fragile shingles and all—something tells me it's meant more for display than play."

"It's—she's—it'll showcase her miniatures," he said miserably. "She collects this tiny scale-model furniture and stuff."

"You're right in the middle of building that thing. It's really beautiful. Don't tell me you're going to abandon it now, after all the work you've put into it."

Even in the low lighting, she saw Brent flush. "I'll finish it," he said, not meeting her eyes. "But that doesn't mean anything. I promised her a dollhouse and she's going to get one."

"So you're going to, what? Give her this elaborate dollhouse you made just for her and say here it is, we're through?"

"How do you know I haven't already told her we're through?"

"Because no self-respecting woman would let you keep working on a project like that after you'd dumped her for another woman. She'd take that fancy dollhouse and smash it over your thick skull."

"I was hoping..." Brent reached for his glass and tossed back half his wine. "I was hoping the dollhouse would kind of soften the blow."

"Like a consolation prize?" Men could be so clueless. "Brent, it isn't the damn dollhouse she wants, it's you!"

"What makes you say that? You don't even know her."

"Unless this Marina is a total dullard, she's as aware of me as I've been of her. Chances are, she's figured out I was there first and she's the other woman."

He emitted something between a whimper and a moan.

Raven asked, "Is she a dullard?"

He shook his head.

She patted his arm. "Then she's waiting you out. Biding her time, hoping you'll come around and realize she's the woman for you. Which shows she's got more emotionally invested in you than I have."

"What does that mean?"

"I don't love you, Brent."

"You think you don't—you're just hurt."

"And you don't love me, either."

"Sure I do, honey. Why do you think I want to marry you?"

"Actually, I'm trying to figure that out. You've been seeing Marina almost as long as you've been seeing me.

You've broken several dates with me to be with her." He opened his mouth and she said, "Don't you dare lie to me, Brent Radley. No more lies."

He threw up his hands. "I told you. I was stupid. My priorities were twisted around. That's in the past."

"Getting you to the club to watch me perform was like pulling teeth, but here you're building Marina a three-story dollhouse complete with little strips of fascia molding and tiny working windows and itty-bitty brass wall sconces that light up, for heaven's sake. You must've invested hundreds of hours in that project so far."

"What's your point?" he grumbled, shoving the ring back into its box.

"Marina's not the other woman. I am."

His gaze shot to her. "It not her I want, it's you."

"Why?"

"Well, because...we're right for each other."

"What makes me so right for you? What do I have that Marina doesn't?"

"Character."

"What's wrong with Marina's character?"

"It's not...there's nothing exactly wrong with her character, it's just that...you have more of it."

"I have more character?"

"That's right. You have more of what I expect in a wife."

Raven pondered his words, taking note of his telling discomfort with this subject, the gaps he seemed so reluctant to fill in. When the truth came to her she had to stifle a huff of laughter.

"It's because I wouldn't sleep with you," she said. "That's it, isn't it?" She sat straighter, her smile incredulous. "I didn't sleep with you and she did, and that made all the difference."

"That's an oversimplification."

"Then what else is there? What are the other differences in our character?"

He sighed in exasperation. "This is a pointless exercise. It's you I—"

"Is she cruel to animals? Does she pick her nose in public?"

"Jeez, Raven. I'm trying to propose to you, for crying out loud!"

"Okay, I'm obviously not very romantic. There's one strike against me."

"This whole thing is a joke to you, isn't it?"

"Sure," she said, deadpan, "it's one big laugh fest. Tell me. What does Marina do for a living?"

With obvious reluctance he said, "She's a swimsuit model."

"Oh. My. God."

"Raven—"

"You cheated on me with a *swimsuit model?*" Visions of *Sports Illustrated*'s recent swimsuit issue bombarded her mind. Wet, nubile young women clad in little more than suntans and goose bumps. The scraps of cloth they modeled had to weigh less than the sand that clung to their skinny thighs and buoyant bosoms and tiny, peachlike behinds.

"How is an ordinary woman supposed to compete with that?" she demanded.

"With what?"

Men!

"With that kind of centerfold perfection, that's what!"

He drew himself up. "For your information, there's more to Marina than her body—she's a nice girl."

"I thought you said she was lacking in character." As he stumbled over a response, Raven continued, "You know, somehow I don't think Marina tied you down and ravished you. I'm betting you pulled out the stops to get her into bed, and now you're condemning her for being 'easy.' You're one of those men who believe there are two kinds of women—the kind you marry and the kind you—"

"Is that what you think of me?" Brent pressed a hand to his chest. "That I hold women to some kind of double standard? What kind of a Neanderthal do you take me for?"

"I have just one question for you, Brent. Who does your gut tell you to spend the rest of your life with—me or Marina?"

"This isn't about my gut."

"Granted, there are other body parts that come into play, but let's stick to one thing at a time. You know what I'm getting at. If you married me, you'd always re- gret it. Because no matter what you say, you don't really love me." She held up her hand to forestall his objection. "You have yet to say those three little words, do you realize that?"

Brent hesitated. Tenderly he stroked her arm; he looked right into her eyes. "Love grows over time, Raven."

"I think you're already in love, and I think you'd realize that *if* you weren't hung up on this 'character' issue. I'm not going to marry you, and if you wait too long to come to your senses about Marina, you'll lose her to some guy who appreciates her and doesn't judge her based on antediluvian notions about wifely purity."

A muscle twitched in his jaw, reminding her of his brother. Last Wednesday she'd refrained from telling Hunter about her pending breakup with Brent, thinking Brent had a right to hear it first, in person. After Hunter had left her so abruptly in her car, during that rainstorm, she'd thought perhaps she should have told him, after all.

But it wouldn't have made any difference—he'd told her he wouldn't have her even if she were no longer with Brent. She'd expected him to take that stand, of course, out of family loyalty; still, hearing him spell it out so ruthlessly had been sobering, to say the least.

Raven wished to God she'd never entered the Wedding Ring pact so long ago. Then she'd never have met Brent or his brother. She wouldn't be suffering this raw, empty ache right now.

She rose. "You'd better turn off the oven. I think that lasagne's beginning to scorch."

Glumly Brent watched her retrieve her coat from the closet. She scooped up her shoulder bag from the floor and walked back to him. "We'll probably never see each other again." She bent to kiss his cheek as she buttoned her coat. "I wish you happiness, Brent. I mean that."

Silently he tracked her progress until she reached the front door. Finally he said, "There's something you should know."

She looked at him expectantly.

"It's about Hunter." He picked up his wineglass. Leaned back on the sofa. Twirled the glass without looking at her. "He's got a thing for you."

She stood paralyzed with her hand on the knob.

"But you probably knew that already." Brent cast her a wry glance. "You seem to have pretty reliable intuition about these things. Anyway, maybe it's the real thing or maybe he's just in lust. If it's the real thing, he's sure as hell not going to tell me, is he?" He finished the last of his wine.

Raven dropped her gaze to the gloves clutched in her hand. "Why are you telling me this?" When he failed to answer, she looked up and saw him studying her.

"It isn't one-sided, is it?" he asked.

No more lies, she'd told Brent. "No," she said quietly. "It isn't one-sided."

"Is he the reason you're...?" He made walking motions with his fingers.

She shook her head. "I told you, Brent. You and I couldn't have made it work. Even if there were no

Hunter. Even if there were no Marina. Trust is very important to me."

He acknowledged this with a small nod. "Well, I'd say that now might be a good time for you to have a little powwow with my brother, but you'll have to track him down first."

Her heart stammered. "What do you mean, track him down?"

"Hunter took off yesterday, for parts unknown," Brent said. "Not long after I showed him the ring."

16

HUNTER SIPPED Glenmorangie Scotch and gazed around at the interior of the Padded Cell. The walls of the club were indeed padded, lined with some sort of bulging, tufted white material. Speakers blasted the discordant strains of "They're Coming to Take Me Away" at migraine-inducing volume. A card on the table listed pricey house-specialty drinks with names like Totally Bonkers and Of Unsound Mind, questionable concoctions that Hunter had eschewed in favor of his usual single-malt whiskey.

The waiters and waitresses wore tops that resembled straitjackets, with their arms free, of necessity, and the leather straps hanging loose. Most of them had gelled their hair into deranged-looking spikes.

Earlier, Hunter had snagged a table for one near the stage and ordered a Loco Burger Deluxe. His waitress, who'd introduced herself as Demented Doris, had asked how he wanted his burger cooked: "crispy around the edges, maddeningly medium, or half-baked?"

"Rare," he'd growled. The lackluster meal had ended with a dessert called Stark Raving Nuts, aka a slice of cloying, dried-out pecan pie.

The owner of this place had taken the goofy theme to extremes. The club was smaller than Stitches, but louder, more frenetic; the sensory overload was downright oppressive. Hunter wouldn't even have come here except that he was determined to do something more constructive with his après-ski hours than sit in his rented room feeling sorry for himself. He figured that visiting the local comedy clubs here in Vermont—"shopping the competition"—qualified as constructive. Not only could he compare the clubs and perhaps get some ideas, but he'd be able to claim at least part of the trip as a tax deduction.

When he thought of it that way, he could almost convince himself he wasn't running away from his problems. He'd told himself it was for Brent and Raven's sake that he'd left Stitches in Matt's hands and hightailed it to Killington for an extended vacation—his first since opening the club. Without him around, Brent and his fiancé stood a better chance of cementing their future. Raven would be able to concentrate on the man she loved without the disrupting presence of his unscrupulous little brother.

Funny, he'd never thought of himself as unscrupulous before Raven had entered his life. Of course, never before had his scruples been so sorely tested.

His first three nights in Vermont had been on the weekend, and the clubs he'd visited had featured semiwell-known headliners. It was now Monday, openmike night at the Padded Cell. The house lights dimmed and a fortyish woman with a striped purple-

and-orange buzz cut and garish makeup strode onto the stage, the backdrop of which was padded like the rest of the club. She wore a doctor's white lab coat and brandished a bullwhip.

Her method of warming up the crowd consisted of screeching things like "Are you ready to go completely in*sane?*" while snapping the whip. She kept it up until she had the rowdier, drunker elements of the audience howling, barking and stomping their feet. One woman in back did an awesomely realistic monkey call at the top of her lungs.

Hunter had seen—and heard—enough. A dull throbbing had begun behind his eyes. Rising, he tossed some money on the table and snatched up his green down vest from the chair back. He turned to leave just as the emcee introduced the first amateur performer.

"You're going to go *crazy* for Raven Muldoon!"

Hunter froze with his back to the stage. He'd misheard. A trick of his Raven-fixated subconscious. Then she spoke, and sure enough, it was Raven's voice saying, "My boyfriend just proposed to me."

Slowly Hunter turned and stared dumbstruck as a smiling Raven, not twenty feet away, tugged the mike out of its stand. She couldn't see him, he knew, with the stage lights in her eyes. Did she know he was there?

Someone behind Hunter griped, "Outta the way, buddy!" but he stood rooted to the spot.

"He bought me a diamond the size of a bottle cap," Raven continued, as the crowd hooted their approval.

"Where's the ring?" yelled a woman in back, and

Hunter looked at Raven's left hand, holding the mike. It was bare.

"I turned him down. I found out he was cheating on me. With a swimsuit model," Raven said, to a mixed chorus of feminine groans and masculine wolf whistles.

The guy behind him snarled, "You gonna move or what?" Hunter dropped back into his seat.

She turned Brent down?

Raven strolled across the stage, gesturing emphatically. "I mean, a swimsuit model! He had to cheat on me with someone who looks sexy flossing her teeth. But that's not the only reason I said no. He's got this—" she stopped in her tracks and gave the audience a sultry smile "—little brother."

This was met with suggestive guffaws and a handful of pithy comments. Hunter could only sit and listen, flabbergasted.

"Yes, it's true," she admitted. "I fell in love with my boyfriend's brother. How tacky is that? It's like sneaking back for seconds and thirds when they're giving away free samples of fried pork rinds at the supermarket—you can't believe you're doing it, you're helpless to stop and you pray to God you don't get caught."

I fell in love with my boyfriend's brother. The words echoed in Hunter's mind. Had she really said them? Did she mean them?

Raven went on to describe, in dryly humorous terms, how she was obligated by the terms of a secret high-school matchmaking pact to date the designated boyfriend for three months, despite the fact that she'd fallen for his brother big-time.

That was why she'd kept seeing Brent! Hunter realized with a start. When she'd told him that she couldn't explain why she was still with Brent despite his cheating, he'd accused her of being blindly in love, a doormat—but it was really because of this bizarre pact she and her pals had concocted when they were kids!

Raven got a lot of laughs describing the debilitating fear of heights that had prompted Hunter to seek private therapy with her, yet somehow had failed to keep him out of swaying ski lifts and rickety little airplanes.

"That was when I began to think maybe I wasn't the only one who liked fried pork rinds," she said.

Her act ended with a couple of gags about relations between the sexes that she'd recycled from her Stitches routines. Hunter was out of his seat before she'd blown her signature parting kiss to the audience. In his haste to intercept her he slalomed around tables in the dimly lit club, nearly knocking over a busboy balancing a tray full of grimy dishes. Onstage, the emcee introduced the next act, a Bobcat Goldthwaite wanna-be who began whining his way through a bizarre routine about road rage.

Just as Hunter reached the stage door, it swung open and Raven stepped out. Now that she was standing there, right in front of him, all he could do was fling his arms out and let his befuddled expression ask what the hell was going on.

"Nice to see you, too," she said, rising on her toes to plant a soft kiss on his mouth.

"Let's get out of here." He grabbed her arm.

"Wait, I've got to get my things. I'll meet you up front."

A half minute later Raven joined Hunter at the club entrance. He helped her into her coat and led her out into the cool, damp night. "Is your car here?" he asked.

"Yeah, it's a rental." She pointed out a blue Corolla parked two rows away. "I flew up."

"Let's take mine."

"Where?" she asked.

"I don't know. Nowhere." He thumbed the remote entry, and the Outback obligingly beeped. "Just get in."

They settled into the front bucket seats. Hunter started the engine but didn't put the vehicle in gear. Sitting parked with Raven outside a comedy club reminded him all too vividly of the last time he'd seen her, five days ago, when he'd abruptly taken off after making love to her—if he could even call that brusque, impulsive act "making love."

"Why did you come here?" he asked.

With quiet sincerity she said, "Because I love you."

Hunter closed his eyes. Her words curled around his heart, swelling his chest, warming him. On some level he'd always known she loved him, even as he'd tried to convince himself—and Raven—that hers was a superficial attraction.

He opened his eyes, stared out the windshield into

the dark night. He forced himself to say, "I told you, Raven. I won't take you from my brother."

"It's not like that." She laid her cold hand over his, where it rested on his thigh. "Brent and I are through."

"Raven—"

"I knew we were through last week, when you and I...when I saw you last. I didn't want to tell you before I told him."

"None of that matters. Don't you understand? It's bad enough I came between you two. If it weren't for me, you and Brent would've made it work—"

Her snort of amusement cut him off. "Hunter, do you think I'd willingly spend the rest of my life with a man I couldn't trust? Weren't you listening in there?" She jerked her head toward the club. "I would've given him the boot as soon as I found out about Marina, if it weren't for the Wedding Ring."

"The Wedding Ring." Despite everything, he had to smile. "You and your pals are certifiable—you know that, don't you?" The engine had warmed enough for him to switch the heater on. Warm air blew from the vents.

"Are we going to sit here all night?" she asked.

After a moment Hunter said, "There's a quiet parlor in the inn where I'm staying. We can talk there."

Her voice held a smile. "You don't trust me enough to take me to your room?"

"It's not you I don't trust," he muttered as he backed out of the parking space. "I can't believe you can even joke about it, after the way I treated you last Wednesday."

"What do you mean?"

"Just for the record, Raven, that wasn't my usual style. I wish I'd..." He sighed. "Well, if it was going to happen, it shouldn't have happened that way. I wasn't thinking, I was just...I don't know what I was doing."

"Well, whatever you were doing, it was pretty damn exciting."

He pulled onto the road. "I was afraid I'd hurt you."

"Like I said. Exciting." She laughed at the dubious look he shot her. "No lasting damage."

He frowned. "Well, I can do better. I didn't even wait for you to finish."

"So how about I give you a chance to make it up to me?"

"This is not a joke, Raven. It can never happen again. You shouldn't have come up here."

"I told you, Brent and I were finished anyway. It had nothing to do with you."

"What about the pact? I thought you had to keep seeing him for another month."

"Forget it. I just rewrote the rules."

He took note of her unyielding expression. "It makes no difference why you broke up with him. He's still my brother. For me to take up with the woman he had his heart set on marrying—"

"And if I told you that it was Brent who sent me after you?"

"What?"

"He contacted all your friends, your folks, everyone, trying to find out where you'd gone. He spent hours on the phone Friday night and Saturday morning."

"My folks? He talked to my folks? Did he tell them about us? You and me?"

"Yep. They were, well, surprised," Raven said, with a wry smile, "but in the end I think they figured if it was okay with Brent, it was okay with them."

"It's okay with Brent," Hunter repeated, awestruck.

"You didn't tell *anyone* where you were off to," Raven continued, "but Brent figured your assistant manager had to know. You wouldn't take chances when it came to the club. Finally he tracked Matt to his girlfriend Jerri's apartment. Apparently you'd sworn him to secrecy. Jerri let slip that you'd gone to Killington, but Matt wouldn't tell him where you were staying. You weren't registered at any of the hotels or motels in the area. I don't ski downhill, so I spent two days haunting the lift lines, the main building, everywhere, trying to spot you. I had you paged, but you never responded."

"I spent most of my time on the meaner slopes." Punishing himself, trying to forget why he'd fled New York.

"I called Brent today, at the end of my rope," she said. "It was his idea to check out the local comedy clubs."

"But how did you know which one I'd be at? There are a few."

"I drove around, scoped out the parking lots. When I

got to the Padded Cell, I spotted your trusty steed." She patted the dashboard.

"Then when you found out it was open-mike night..." He chuckled, incredulous. "You went through all that, just to run me to ground?"

"Well, no one knew when you were coming back—not even Matt. I was afraid you were determined to hide out until Brent and I had tied the knot and started filling a minivan with 2.3 kids."

"Brent really did that? Helped track me down so you and I could be together? I find that hard to believe."

"Your brother loves you, Hunter. He wants you to be happy. He knows how I feel about you. And he knows you...feel something for me."

Hunter heard the question in her voice. What courage it must have taken for Raven to lay her heart bare, not just before him but before the entire rowdy audience at the Padded Cell, with no guarantee that he returned her love. An hour ago, he'd thought he had this whole mess figured out, had resigned himself to maintaining a polite distance from his sister-in-law for the rest of his life. Now he grappled with this latest, remarkable development, hardly daring to believe it was true, that Raven could be his, that Brent not only approved but had taken an active role in getting them together.

Raven said, "You can call him if you don't believe me."

"I don't think you're lying, angel, I just... It's all just a little overwhelming." Hunter swung the car into the gravel drive of the Wilton Street Inn, a sprawling yellow clapboard house built in the last century. He looked at Raven, at her sweetly earnest expression, her tender smile. "Did you really give him back his ring?"

"I never accepted it in the first place. Let him save it for Marina."

Hunter chewed back a grin. "I've seen the ring. Something tells me it's not Marina's style. And anyway, Brent has no intention of marrying her."

"Oh, I think he may surprise you."

"More surprises? Why didn't I see that one coming?" He found a spot in the parking area behind the house and cut the engine and headlights. Little light from the full moon made it into the car. He felt more than saw Raven—sensed her warmth, her fragrance. "Speaking of surprises—you know, I didn't use anything. You could be pregnant."

"Well, then, you'll just have to marry me."

A crack of laughter burst from Hunter. God, it felt good to laugh. "Try and stop me. And if you're not pregnant, we'll just have to keep working on it." Startled by his own impulsive words, he asked softly, "How do you feel about that?"

"Are you asking me if I want to have a baby?" she breathed. "Your baby?"

Hunter reached across the darkness separating them. He stroked her satiny cheek. "I love you, Raven. I love you and I need you and dammit, let's get married! Soon. We don't have to wait until there's a baby on the way."

"A wedding first," she said with a laugh. "What a novel concept. What about Stitches?"

"That's a great idea! We've done private parties at the club, but never a wedding."

"No, I mean—I thought you weren't interested in marriage," she said as they let themselves out of the car. "You told me the club was all the responsibility you could handle at one time."

"And you listened to me?" He slid his arm around her back and steered her toward the inn's side entrance. "I was young and foolish. And I'd never been in love."

"Yeah, about that young part..."

"What?"

"Doesn't it bother you? That I'm so much older?"

"This is a joke, right?" He opened the door and ushered her into the hallway off the kitchen, invitingly warm and perfumed with the rich, yeasty aromas of baking. He heard Mrs. Strange, the innkeeper, warbling off-key in the kitchen, accompanying Lyle Lovett on her radio. Muted conversation drifted from the public rooms as Hunter led Raven toward the wide curved stairway with its thick burgundy carpeting and polished oak banister.

"Is this the way to that nice quiet parlor?" she asked with a crooked grin.

"No, it's the way to my nice private room. Don't change the subject. What's with this 'so much older' stuff?"

"Four years," she said. "That's a significant difference."

"To who? Raven, there are four years between you and Brent, too. I didn't see either of you getting worked up over it."

"That's—" She broke off.

"Different? Why? Because no one thinks anything if the guy is older, that's why. It's expected."

"You're used to perky young girls," she grumbled, following him down the second-floor hallway as he fished the room key from his pocket. "Like Kirsten."

Laughing, Hunter opened the door. "After everything, you still need reassurance that I find you sexy and desirable? That if I live to be a hundred and twenty, I'll still find you sexy and desirable?" Hooking his arm around Raven's waist, he unceremoniously hauled her into the room and slammed the door shut.

17

WITHOUT WARNING, Hunter lifted Raven and deposited her on the nearby low dresser, a fussy antique piece crafted of glossy dark wood and topped with a crocheted lace runner she could just make out in the moonlight pouring in through sheer window curtains. Her senses whirled as he kissed her with breathtaking intensity, stepping between her legs and pulling her hard against him, causing her trench coat and her long, slate blue skirt to ride up her legs.

Urgent little sounds bubbled up her throat as she kissed him back. He groaned and pressed closer, the ridge of his erection nudging her through their clothing.

"You're pretty hot for an old broad," he teased, chuckling when she retaliated with a solid whack on his shoulder. He stripped off his down vest and tossed it across the room onto the braided rug next to the high four-poster, double bed. Next he shed his beige flannel shirt, leaving him in a charcoal-gray turtleneck and jeans. Unfastening the buttons of her trench coat, he said, "Here's a radical idea. How about this time I get you out of this thing first?"

"Out of a whole lot more than that, I hope."

The look Hunter gave her could have melted steel.

Pale moonlight glinted in his dark hair and picked out the bold planes and angles of his face. He pushed the coat off her and kissed her again, slower this time, and deeper. The galloping tattoo of his heartbeat made her dizzy. So did his heat, the scent of his skin, the repressed power she detected in his every movement. Even his abrasive beard stubble inflamed her.

He kneed her legs farther apart, widening his stance as if he meant to take her right there on the dresser top. His long fingers splayed over her scalp as his tongue plunged and retreated, tasting, promising.

Finally he broke off with a ragged moan. "We've got to slow down. I don't want a repeat of last Wednesday."

"Maybe next time," Raven said.

A lopsided smile split his face. "You really liked seeing me lose control, didn't you?"

She wrenched his turtleneck out of the waistband of his jeans and pulled it up. Obligingly he raised his arms and helped tug it over his head. Raven had never seen Hunter's bare torso before. She stroked her fingers up his forearms, liberally covered with soft, dark hair, to the sinewy smoothness of his upper arms. Her fingertips traced a ropy vein before moving on to his shoulders, hard with muscle.

He stood still as she explored his body, watching her, his expression endearingly patient, but with a smoldering undercurrent that revved her pulse.

Raven caressed Hunter's firm chest, scraping her nails lightly through the wedge of hair and around the flat nipples, delighting in his breathy chuckle. She followed the trail of hair down his tight belly to his navel, just peeking out of his pants.

"My turn." He reached for the slate-blue V-neck sweater.

"Not yet." Raven slid off the dresser and unbuckled his belt. She'd spent two long months wondering what Hunter looked like without his clothes, and as far as she was concerned, the wait was over. She let him yank off his scuffed leather boots and socks, then she divested him of his jeans.

Underneath he wore snug-fitting, gray knit boxer shorts that clung to his lean hips and brawny thighs. He looked so good in the boxers that she would have been tempted to let him keep them on, if it weren't for a certain eye-catching bulge that commanded her attention.

"Allow me." She knelt and slipped her fingers into the white elastic waistband.

Smiling, he lifted his arms away from his sides. "Be my guest."

Raven's heart fluttered in her throat as she carefully worked the stretchy fabric over the rigid column of his penis and down his legs. The sense of womanly power was intoxicating, but no more so than the realization that this remarkable man wanted her not just for tonight but for a lifetime.

She rose and, with a soft laugh, slipped out of his reach. "Not that I think there are any Peeping Toms in the neighborhood, but..." She drew the shades under the sheer curtains, ensuring their privacy. Crossing to the nightstand, she touched the switch on the small table lamp. "Do you mind?"

"Of course not."

Raven turned on the lamp, casting the room in a soft light. Hunter displayed no self-consciousness as she stared at him, despite his flagrant state of arousal. It wasn't that he was vain, she realized; he was simply comfortable in his skin. He looked like a young god standing before her, strong and straight and heart-breakingly handsome.

"You're...magnificent," she whispered, and he smiled as if to say, *And you're biased*. "Do you think I'm awful, just wanting to look at you?"

"As long as that's not all you want to do."

"Not by a long shot." She unfastened her skirt and let it fall.

Hunter's gaze zeroed in on her legs. "I've got to tell you, you look incredible in those."

Raven looked down at herself. Her sweater ended at her hips, exposing a generous expanse of skin above the lacy tops of her black, thigh-high stockings. "The boots don't spoil the effect?"

"I don't know. Why don't you lose them and I'll tell you."

She pulled off her brown suede half boots.

He rubbed his chin consideringly. "Still hard to say. You'd better take off the sweater, too."

With an impish smile, she pulled the sweater over her head and dropped it. She'd never been one for sexy lin-gerie, and now she wished she owned something more alluring than this floral-printed cotton bra and matching bikini panties. "There," she said. "Does that help?"

If Hunter found her underthings dowdy, he gave no indication. On the contrary, he was rampantly aroused, obviously reining himself in. Seeing him this way, with that feral look in his eye, stoked Raven's own excitement. Every womanly part of her hummed with awareness.

As if in slow motion, he closed the distance between them. He lifted a hand and trailed one finger from the hollow of her throat down her chest to lightly skim her cleavage. A small sound escaped Raven. Her breasts felt almost unbearably sensitized. He reached around her back, unhooked her bra and slipped the straps off her shoulders, letting it fall to their feet.

"This is like a dream." His expression was one of wonderment as he lightly touched her breasts, tracing their shape. "All this time, wanting you so badly, needing you so much and knowing you could never be mine. And now here you are—and there's nothing to keep us apart. I feel like any minute now I'm going to wake up and find out this really is all a dream."

Raven slid her arms around his neck and stepped into his embrace. "Then I'm dreaming that I'm about to share myself with the man I love. I'm dreaming that I've never been happier." She pressed closer, until her breasts were flattened against his chest, and the satiny steel of his erection prodded her belly. His fingers swept down her bare back and under the edge of her panties. She shivered as he caressed her. "I'm dreaming that if you wait much longer to make love to me, I'm going to lose my mind."

His response was a frustrated chuckle. "If you only knew how hard I'm trying not to throw you on that bed and ravish you..."

She kissed him. "Maybe I'll do the ravishing this time." She turned them around and backed him toward the bed.

"And maybe I'll let you."

Grinning, she said, "If you 'let' me, it wouldn't be ravishment, would it?" With a burst of strength she pushed him onto the bed and leaped on top of him, pressing his shoulders to the ecru crocheted bedspread. His legs hung over the edge.

The corners of his eyes crinkled. "I suppose it will do me no good to beg for mercy."

"None at all. My mind's made up." She bent lower until her breasts just grazed his chest. She kissed his throat, his collarbone, gradually moving lower, teasing them both with sinuous movements of her body.

Hunter's chest rose and fell faster. His hands moved restlessly over her, everywhere he could reach. Raven rejoiced in his broken sighs, his heated murmurs. She kissed her way down his torso, over his corrugated abdomen. Sliding down to kneel on the braided rug, she brushed her cheek against his rigid penis.

"Raven!" His fingers tangled in her hair as he half rose. His voice was hoarse with strain. "Angel, don't. I won't last if you do that."

She pushed him down, forcefully, and he fell back

with a defeated little laugh. She trailed her fingertips down his hips and powerful legs, stroking up his inner thighs on the return movement, briefly touching the potent fullness there. She repeated the caress over and over until Hunter was writhing. His color was high; veins stood out in his neck.

His arousal was spectacular to behold. A dewdrop glistened on the tip, and she touched it, gently spread it. His hips jerked and his breath snagged. Bolting upright, he seized her wrist and held her away from him.

"That's enough," he rasped.

"It's not nearly enough."

"You know what I mean, you witch." Hunter's eyes glittered with amusement and steely determination as he pulled her up and tossed her onto the bed.

"I thought it was my turn to ravish," she said as he pinned her down.

"There's a fine line between ravishment and torture, and you crossed it, angel. Now you'll have to pay the price."

This was going to be anything but a boring marriage, Raven reflected as she took note of her lover's devilish smile. He lifted her right knee and began working the sheer black stocking down her leg.

"I thought you liked me in these," she said.

"I have other plans for them."

Raven's pulse jumped. "Are you going to tie me up?"

He regarded the four tall bedposts with interest. "Not this time."

Hunter lifted her lower leg and pulled the toe of the

stocking, which slid off her calf with a whisper of sound. He studied the filmy fabric, drew it through his fingers. "This is real silk, isn't it?"

She nodded. "My one extravagance. Um, what are you going to do?" she asked as he stripped the other stocking off her.

"To tell you the truth, I'm not entirely sure myself. I could pull it over my head and we could play cops and robbers. No? Just an idea."

She shivered with sensual anticipation as he sat next to her and looked her over from head to toe, as if pondering his next move. Finally he said, "Turn over."

After a moment's hesitation, she rolled onto her stomach. The rough crocheted bedspread excited her sensitized nipples. He lifted her arms and arranged them comfortably over her head, before reclining on his side next to her. She watched him double the stocking, forming a loop.

He said, "Close your eyes."

She looked at him, and at the stocking.

"Go on," he said. "Close your eyes."

She did.

"Relax..." he whispered.

She laughed. "That's usually my line."

A few seconds later, a butterfly alighted on her big toe. "Oh...!" Her eyes flashed open; she craned her neck and saw Hunter dangling the silk stocking over her foot.

"No peeking," he said, and kissed her eyes closed. The butterfly flitted up her calf and lingered on the inside of her knee before continuing its upward path, stopping at the top of her thigh.

"Let's get rid of these." Hunter hooked his fingers over the edge of her panties. Raven was unprepared for the startling feeling of exposure when he pulled them off her. "That's better," he said, and added warmly, "much better."

She dragged in an unsteady breath. "Hunter—"

"Shh." The butterfly touched down on her waist. It played over her back, flirted with the sides of her breasts. With an effort, Raven managed not to move. The stocking danced down her spine to her buttocks, where it skittered over the twin globes and between them, sending shafts of pleasure through her.

He dragged the stocking down her legs and up them, concentrating on her tender inner thighs, returning to her bottom again and again. Urgent little sighs escaped Raven and she lost the battle to lie still. Her intimate flesh felt heavy, moisture-laden; her hips rocked under the silky caress. Every instinct screamed at her to turn over and pull Hunter down on top of her.

As if he'd read her mind, he said, "Turn over."

She did. Again he raised her arms. "Can I open my eyes now?" she asked.

"No."

Raven bit back a gasp when the butterfly landed on her navel. It sketched figure eights on her quivering belly before changing course and fluttering up her rib cage. All sensation converged on the point of contact as it circled her left breast and proceeded up her sensitive armpit and the underside of her arm.

The silk trailed up her hand and glanced off her fingertips. Then nothing. Eyes closed, she held her breath, wondering what part of her would receive attention next.

A tingling current shot through her right nipple. She arched half off the bed. Hunter tickled her breasts with the silk, dragging it from tip to tip, lightly stroking, varying the pressure and the speed.

"Hunter, it's...ohh..." she moaned, squirming. "Let me open my eyes," she pleaded.

His voice was a sensual rumble. "Not yet."

"I can't take any more!"

She heard his smile when he replied, "Oh, sure you can."

He abandoned her breasts at last, to slowly drag the stocking down her torso. It dallied with her hips, her thighs, the triangle of curls, skipping from one spot to the next until Raven was panting softly, clutching fistfuls of the bedspread. Her hips twitched restlessly.

At last he knelt between her legs, pushing them wide, and she failed to restrain a whimper of longing. Eyes still closed, she felt more exposed than ever, open and vulnerable and racked by a clawing hunger that robbed her of all self-control.

Please, she silently begged. *Please, oh please, oh please. Damn it, now!*

She waited, listening to her own rasping breaths, her rushing pulse. Without warning, a thrill of sensation flared between her legs. Her eyes snapped open. She cried out, bucking off the bed, only to have Hunter's palm come down hard on her waist as he repeatedly drew the delicate stocking over her most sensitive parts. She fought his restraining hand, struggled in vain to close her legs, a reflexive response to pleasure so acute it was nearly unendurable.

Raw, blinding need coiled tighter and tighter, until she knew she was going to come, felt it gathering swift and sharp within her, tugging at her insides, rearing up like a beast of prey—

Hunter raised her hips and plunged into her in one long, slow, searing stroke. Raven's orgasm ripped through her, blossoming like a fireball, consuming her. He stoked it with short, fierce thrusts until she collapsed, limp, under him.

He was still hard, gorging her, nudging the womanly depths of her. She pushed up against him, and he pressed her into the mattress, holding her still.

"Do me a favor, angel," he growled into her ear. "Don't move."

Even in her dazed state she was aware of the tension in his body, the sheer will he exerted to delay his own climax. He pressed soft kisses to her temple, her throat and shoulder. After a minute he began moving once more.

She was transfixed by Hunter's eyes, the burning intensity of his expression as he loved her slowly, advancing, receding, kindling her desire anew. She found herself enchanted by the sweet, shining oneness of it, and knew he felt it, too. It was more than sex, more than the culmination of two months of bittersweet longing. It was right and proper, their love; it was meant to be.

They moved as one, a fluid dance punctuated by sighs and whispered intimacies. They reached the peak as one, clinging to each other afterward in breathless, boneless repletion.

Raven lay in Hunter's arms, listening to the muted sounds of the busy inn. A door slamming downstairs. A pair of young girls laughing and running in the hall-way. A car pulling up in the gravel drive outside.

Hunter stroked her arm. "Are you cold?"

"Mmm-hmm." She wasn't, really, but the thought of snuggling between the sheets with Hunter was too delicious to resist.

He pulled the covers down and over them both. Raven indulged herself in a voluptuous, full-body stretch.

Hunter propped himself on an elbow. He wore the sweetest, sexiest smile. "You look very pleased with yourself."

"I feel very pleased with myself."

"Well, I *am* quite the catch, it's true."

"And the soul of modesty."

He lifted one of her stockings from the bedspread and dragged it across her breasts. "Did you enjoy this?"

"I hated it. Couldn't you tell?"

"Mmm, yes, all that groaning and carrying on. I should've known."

Raven snatched the stocking from him.

He arched an eyebrow. "What are you up to?"

"Does the phrase 'a taste of your own medicine' mean anything to you?"

"Gee, I'm not sure." He gave her a roguish smile and scooped her into his arms. "You'd better demonstrate."

"Oh, my goodness," she said, when they were belly to belly.

"What?"

"You're already...ready. Again."

He shrugged as if to say, *What did you expect?*

Raven reflected that there were certain unforeseen advantages to marrying a younger man.

"Very well, I'll demonstrate." She tickled his chest with the silk stocking. "But pay attention."

Epilogue

IT WAS AWFULLY SWEET of Hunter and Raven to invite her parents and grandmother to their spring bash, Charli thought as she settled her family at a table near the aisle that had been cleared in the middle of Stitches. They were among the last to arrive; the place was already filled with a couple of hundred partygoers. Hunter and Raven must have invited nearly everyone they knew! Sunny and Amanda and their folks were seated nearby.

It was the first of April, and the club had been decorated in a sunny springtime motif, with yellow gingham tablecloths, cheerful hand-painted dishes—everything matching for a change—pairs of gold taper candles, and baskets brimming with bright green mint and yellow flowers: orchids, roses, Solomon's seal and honeysuckle. Even the stage was festooned with flowers.

"What kind of music is that?" Grandma Rossi asked, as Charli pushed in her chair and placed her cane within reach. A deejay had set up in a corner of the room, near a portable wooden dance floor.

"I think it's called jazz fusion," Charli said.

Grandma said, "I thought it was R and B."

"I hope it doesn't get louder," Papa groused.

Mama said, "It's not loud!"

"I didn't say it was loud! I said I hoped it didn't get louder, Betty. Get your hearing checked!"

"*Basta!*" Grandma scolded. "Listen to you two old fools, fussing like children!"

"I'm hungry," Papa said. "Aren't they going to feed us?"

"Joey!" Grandma tossed up her hand. "You just ate lunch!"

"I'm hungry!"

"Look, Joe." Mama pointed out a waitress with a laden tray. "They're coming around with nibble food. You won't starve."

"I have to ask Sunny...something," Charli lied, eager for a few minutes' respite from her contentious family. "I'll be right back."

The music stopped. "At this time everyone will kindly find their seats," the deejay announced.

Charli sank into her chair. Escape would have to wait. Hunter and Raven probably wanted to officially greet their guests.

Sure enough, Hunter emerged from behind the stage, looking dapper in a dark gray, double-breasted suit— but where was Raven? His brother, Brent, joined him, along with Raven's sister, Lenore, and a round middle-aged woman with a dramatic shock of white in her chestnut hair. She was wearing a black robe that almost looked like a—

It was. A clerical robe! A murmur rose among the assembled guests, swiftly turning to stunned gasps as the deejay started playing the wedding march. The crowd turned in unison toward the back of the room, where Raven stood, flanked by her parents. They must have slipped in from the nearby kitchen.

Mama and Papa gaped at the bride. Sunny let out a delighted squeal that carried throughout the room. From her table nearby, Amanda stage-whispered to Charli, "Did you know?"

Grinning, giggling, feeling her eyes fill with tears of joy, Charli shook her head. "I had no idea. I thought this was just a party!"

"This wedding better be the real thing," Amanda hissed. "If it's their idea of an April Fool's joke, I'll kill them!"

"Ha!" With a gleeful cackle, Grandma slapped the table. "My little bird got herself a husband!"

"This is no place to get married!" Mama glanced around, bug-eyed. "They should be in a church!"

Charli shushed her family and turned her attention to Raven as she and her parents began the slow procession down the aisle to her waiting groom. Her calf-length gown—a sheer, straight, short-sleeved sheath layered over an opaque slip dress in the same warm champagne hue—evoked the 1920s.

The bodice and fluttery hem were trimmed in antique-looking lace. Her hair was swept up in a soft French twist, with strands left loose to wave around her face. She carried a small clutch of yellow pansies and a look of such serene happiness, she practically glowed.

As did Hunter. His eyes never once left his bride during her long trek down the aisle. A small set of steps had been placed in front of the stage. Raven paused there to exchange warm hugs with her mother and father, who took their places at a table in front with Hunter's parents. Hunter extended his hand to escort Raven onto the stage, and twined her fingers with his as they faced the minister.

Lenore, Raven's matron of honor, by all appearances, beamed from ear to ear. Brent, too, appeared genuinely happy in his role as best man—no surprise to Charli, who knew he had long ago given Hunter and Raven his blessing, and was deeply smitten with his own fiancé, Marina.

The minister spoke up. "I've been on this stage before, so I know the drill. If that traffic light in the back starts flashing the one-minute warning, this is going to be the fastest wedding in history."

The actual wedding service, once it began, was as reverent and touching as any Charli had witnessed—although she knew her parents considered anything short of High Mass in a church blasphemy.

Grandma Rossi, on the other hand, hauled out her hand-tatted hankie and dabbed away happy tears. As Lenore read aloud a lengthy poem she'd composed for the couple, Grandma leaned closer to Charli and whispered, "It's your turn now, Carlotta."

"Nonni!" Charli looked around to make sure no one had overheard.

"You turn thirty this week. Now your friends, they find you a husband. It's your turn."

Charli's palms sweated. *My turn*, she thought. How could it be her turn when she was a thirty-year-old virgin who would never be pretty enough or outgoing enough or intriguing enough to hold a man's interest? Any matchmaking attempt on her behalf was destined to be an exercise in humiliation.

She didn't say that. What she said was, "I don't want a husband, Nonni. Who would take care of you and Mama and Papa if I left to get married?"

"Always you think about duty, never about yourself. You're a good girl, Carlotta, but sometimes you gotta think about yourself." She paused meaningfully. "Even when it's a lot less scary to think about duty."

The wedding service resumed then and Charli was left to ponder her grandmother's words as Hunter and Raven exchanged vows that would bind them for the rest of their lives. Watching them, seeing the way they looked at each other, Charli didn't doubt they would indeed be together the rest of their lives.

What must it be like, she wondered, to have a man look at you like that, want you like that? Would she ever find out? Was she brave enough to try? Or was it, as Grandma Rossi had hinted, easier, safer, to cling to duty and live out her life as her parents' mousy, obedient youngest daughter?

The instant they were pronounced husband and wife, Hunter claimed the traditional kiss, which turned decidedly untraditional as he lifted Raven in his arms, still locked mouth to mouth. The guests surged to their feet, clapping and cheering wildly.

Everyone settled down as servers distributed glasses of champagne. A series of impromptu toasts ensued, none more moving than Brent's. He talked about how, when he was twelve and Hunter still a toddler, he'd showed him how to catch fireflies in a mayonnaise jar. Two years later, Hunter surprised their parents by demonstrating his skill at tying his red canvas sneakers, thanks to Brent. In the ensuing years, Brent taught his little brother how to throw a curve ball, change a flat and keep from losing his shirt at the craps table.

"I mean, there I was," Brent continued, "eight years older. The expert. But somewhere along the line, while I was teaching him how to get into R-rated movies and chug a beer in under half a minute, Hunter was figuring out the really important stuff on his own. Like how to know when you're in love—when it's the real McCoy." Brent's voice cracked with emotion. "He didn't get that from me. The truth is, my baby brother here has managed to pound a thing or two into *my* thick skull."

He gave Hunter a huge hug. He hugged his new sister-in-law, too, kissed her cheek and whispered something that made her smile.

"This is the dog that strayed?" Grandma Rossi asked, regarding Brent with a critical eye.

"That's him," Charli said.

"Eh! This one will keep a leash on him," she predicted, nodding toward a gorgeous willowy, black-haired woman who commandeered Brent the instant he was off the stage. She could only be Marina.

Charli didn't ask how her grandmother could foretell

such a thing just from looking at the couple. Perhaps it was body language. Perhaps a look in the eye. No matter. If Luisa Rossi said this was the woman who could put an end to Brent Radley's alley-catting, then by God, this was the woman.

Charli was gratified to see Raven and Marina exchange a warm hug. After all, they were going to be sisters-in-law, or something like that, once Marina and Brent tied the knot. They'd planned an extravagant spring wedding followed by a monthlong honeymoon cruise. Hunter and Raven, by contrast, were leaving tomorrow for England, where they would spend two weeks visiting his relatives, chowing down on pub food and taking in a play or two in London.

"Are they serving a meal," Papa griped around a mouthful of shrimp cocktail, "or is it just this finger food?"

"You and your stomach!" Mama snapped. "What did Dr. Berman say about your cholesterol?"

"Let *Dr. Berman* starve."

Charli said, "I'm sure they're serving a full meal, Papa."

Mama lowered her voice. "We don't have a check for Raven and Hunter."

"Of course we don't have a check!" Papa bellowed. "We didn't know we were going to a wedding! You can't expect presents if you're going to surprise everybody. I'll bet they didn't think about that."

Charli said, "I don't think Raven and Hunter are that interested in presents, Papa. I think they just wanted to share their special day with the people they care about." She caught Sunny's eye, and Amanda's. The three shared an unspoken exchange and stood in unison.

"I'm going to go congratulate them," Charli said, and beat a hasty retreat with Sunny and Amanda to the front of the room. The instant Raven spied her best friends, she launched into a jumble of hugs, kisses and laughter.

Charli, Sunny and Amanda bestowed congratulatory kisses on Hunter, who wore a puckish smile as he said, "I trust you're not too disappointed that things didn't work out exactly as planned."

Sunny's jaw dropped. "Raven! You told him about the pact?"

"You weren't supposed to do that," Charli admonished.

"Correction." Raven raised a finger. "I wasn't supposed to tell the guy I was set up with. We never said anything about the guy's brother."

"Well, the important thing is that it all worked out," Amanda said. "All's well that ends well and all that."

Raven drew her pals into a private huddle. "I know I wasn't into this whole matchmaking thing at first. And I know things got kind of mixed up along the way, but Amanda's right. It all worked out better than I could have imagined. I just want you guys to know—" her eyes got misty "—I'm so grateful to you. Without that crazy Wedding Ring pact, I'd never have met Hunter."

Sunny said, "One down, three to go."

"Two," Amanda corrected. "I'm no longer part of this deal, remember? I've had more than my share of husbands."

Raven arched an eyebrow. "We'll deal with that issue when the time comes. Meanwhile..."

All three turned to Charli.

She swallowed hard. "I've been thinking about it. I don't really want to meet anyone. I mean, I can't get married. Mama and Papa need me—and my grandma—"

"What is it with you guys?" Sunny demanded. "First Raven and now you. I *know* you want to get married, Charli."

Charli felt her face heat. "I've changed my mind."

"That's not the way it works," Sunny reminded her. "Remember what you told Raven when she tried to back out? That we made a promise to each other. We've never broken our promises, you said, and you were right."

"But Amanda's backing out!" Charli objected.

"Amanda *thinks* she's backing out," Raven said, spearing the obstinate divorcé with a significant look.

Sunny said, "I think it's time to invoke the chicken clause." She, Raven and Amanda started flapping their elbows and clucking.

"Stop it!" Charli fretted, as everyone within earshot turned to stare. They didn't stop, but clucked all the louder.

Hunter strolled over to them. "Is this some bizarre bridal ritual I'm not supposed to witness?"

"It's Charli's turn to get a husband," Sunny explained, "and she's trying to chicken out."

Charli dropped her burning face into her hands, mortified when Hunter slid his arm around her shoulders. He leaned in close and spoke for her ears only. "There's no use fighting it, Carlotta. This is a pretty determined bunch, and I have a feeling they're not about to take no for an answer."

She looked at him then, finding his expression one of such warm empathy that she felt her courage ratchet up a notch.

He said, "I also have a feeling that whoever you end up with is going to be a very lucky man."

Charli knew he was just trying to be nice, but he was right about one thing. Her pals weren't about to let her out of the pact. And perhaps Nonni was right when she accused Charli of taking the coward's way out.

She didn't want to be Nonni's age, looking back on a lonely, duty-filled life, regretting that she'd let her one opportunity for happiness slip through her fingers.

Charli took a deep breath. She lifted her chin. "All right," she said. "Find me a husband."

* * *

Don't forget to look out for
I DO, BUT HERE'S THE CATCH
by Pamela Burford
next month.

Modern Romance™
...seduction and
passion guaranteed

Tender Romance™
...love affairs that
last a lifetime

Sensual Romance™
...sassy, sexy and
seductive

Blaze™
...sultry days and
steamy nights

Medical Romance™
...medical drama on
the pulse

Historical Romance™
...rich, vivid and
passionate

29 new titles every month.

*With all kinds of Romance for
every kind of mood...*

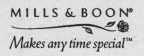

MILLS & BOON®

Makes any time special™

MAT4

2 FREE

books and a surprise gift!

We would like to take this opportunity to thank you for reading this Mills & Boon® book by offering you the chance to take TWO more specially selected titles from the Sensual Romance™ series absolutely FREE! We're also making this offer to introduce you to the benefits of the Reader Service™—

★ FREE home delivery
★ FREE gifts and competitions
★ FREE monthly Newsletter
★ Exclusive Reader Service discounts
★ Books available before they're in the shops

Accepting these FREE books and gift places you under no obligation to buy, you may cancel at any time, even after receiving your free shipment. Simply complete your details below and return the entire page to the address below. *You don't even need a stamp!*

YES! Please send me 2 free Sensual Romance books and a surprise gift. I understand that unless you hear from me, I will receive 4 superb new titles every month for just £2.49 each, postage and packing free. I am under no obligation to purchase any books and may cancel my subscription at any time. The free books and gift will be mine to keep in any case.

T1ZEA

Ms/Mrs/Miss/Mr ....Initials................................
                                                        BLOCK CAPITALS PLEASE
Surname ....
Address ....

....
....Postcode................................

Send this whole page to:
UK: FREEPOST CN81, Croydon, CR9 3WZ
EIRE: PO Box 4546, Kilcock, County Kildare (stamp required)